"Get down!"

The truck's passenger leaned out and aimed again. Randee accelerated, ignoring the detour and veering around it, and merged onto the highway. The passenger fired two more rounds. Shots pinged off her SUV.

She cleared the sign by inches. The truck didn't have enough room to follow, and Randee sped away.

"Is this ever going to end?" Ace barked.

Randee longed to tell him yes. They had to get to the gala with Malte. In the meantime, she needed to ensure they'd lost the truck.

Finally, Randee pulled up to Ace's apartment. She spotted the ATF undercover van parked around the corner. "I won't take long to get ready. How about if I return in an hour to pick you up for the gala?"

"Sure. Thanks." Ace shoved open the door, paused and faced her. "I'm sorry, Randee. I don't mean to be rude. I just don't know how to process all of this."

"I'm sure it'll be over soon." And that was one promise she intended to keep. Tonight.

Sharee Stover is a Colorado native transplanted to Nebraska, where she lives with her husband, three children and two dogs. Her mother instilled in her the love of books before Sharee could read, along with the promise, "If you can read, you can do anything." When she's not writing, she enjoys time with her family, long walks with her obnoxiously lovable German shepherd and crocheting. Find her at shareestover.com or on Twitter, @shareestover.

Books by Sharee Stover

Love Inspired Suspense

Secret Past
Silent Night Suspect
Untraceable Evidence

Untraceable Evidence

Sharee Stover

LOVE INSPIRED SUSPENSE
INSPIRATIONAL ROMANCE

LOVE INSPIRED® SUSPENSE
INSPIRATIONAL ROMANCE

ISBN-13: 978-1-335-40283-7

Recycling programs
for this product may
not exist in your area.

Untraceable Evidence

This edition published by arrangement with Harlequin Books S.A.

For questions and comments about the quality of this book, please contact us at CustomerService@Harlequin.com.

Love Inspired
22 Adelaide St. West, 40th Floor
Toronto, Ontario M5H 4E3, Canada
www.Harlequin.com

Printed in U.S.A.

To the praise of the glory of his grace,
wherein he hath made us accepted in the beloved.
—*Ephesians* 1:6

For the one exhausted from striving for perfection
and approval, know this: you are accepted
in the Beloved and His grace covers you.

Acknowledgments

Many thanks to:

My incredible editor, Emily Rodmell,
whose wisdom and ideas bring out the best
in every story. I am honored to work with you.

To my husband and children. You make life good,
and I love you beyond words.

To my crime writing and solving partners, Connie, Jackie,
Rhonda and Sherrinda, for their perfectly timed icing.

To my agent, Tamela Hancock Murray, for her
willingness to answer all my ridiculous questions.

Most of all, thank You, Father God,
for lavishing Your incredible grace on us.

ONE

ATF special agent Miranda Jareau had her eyes target-locked on Ace Steele, her Glock ready as she watched for possible threats. The man whistled along to whatever tune played in the earbuds peeking from beneath his mass of dark curls, oblivious to the covert security detail.

Randee had backed her vehicle into the space to protect Steele as she readied for her undercover assignment. She sat strategically positioned to ensure unhindered visibility of PrimeRight Laboratory's underground parking garage. Her early reconnaissance allowed her to account for the other vehicles while awaiting Steele's arrival.

She studied the attractive scientist, comparing his appearance against her case file again. She'd anticipated a gawky member of the intelligentsia. Instead, Ace Steele resembled a *GQ* model. The only consistent and accurate similarity to the file was the man's dark-framed glasses. Either he wasn't photogenic, or his surveillance pictures did him no justice.

Though the October morning was considerably warmer than usual for this time of year, Steele wore a buttoned tweed sports coat straining across his broad shoulders and brown Dockers emphasizing his trim waist. The unique silver metal briefcase, containing the specifications for the top secret 3-D printer gun, code named Ghost, swung casually from his hand.

Her phone vibrated, and she glanced down to read the text from her commanding officer, Special Agent in Charge Sergio Vargas. Advise status.

Target approaching lab. Randee responded.

Check in at 10:30.

10-4.

The ATF had vetted all fifty PrimeRight employees prior to the Project Ghost agreement. Only five, including Randee, had clearance to the main area and prototype. Randee's team suspected Titus Malte would be their greatest enemy. Malte's criminal career included avid support and connection with a local militia.

The ATF's surveillance had uncovered communication between an unidentified party at PrimeRight and Malte. Another reason for her undercover assignment. None of the PrimeRight personnel had traceable connections to Malte; however, surveillance had determined a mole existed within the company.

Voice-altering software disguised the callers' identities in every communication, creating an additional obstacle for her team's technical expert, Ishi Haramoto. But Randee had no doubt she would identify them. In the meantime, Sergio had wanted an insider to ferret out the spy and keep an eye on all the parties involved.

The partners were the obvious suspects since they'd have the most to gain, but that was too easy. "The butler did it" type of thinking. If the spy was a trusted member of the PrimeRight employees, he or she was a traitor and didn't deserve to breathe free air.

With one final survey of the garage, Randee concealed her department-issued weapon inside her oversize tote. She contemplated leaving the bag unzipped for quick retrieval, but she couldn't chance Steele seeing the gun.

Annoyance at the pencil skirt and matching blazer she had to wear for this assignment threatened to put her on edge again, but she shoved it down. She'd conduct her mission with the same professionalism and excellence she did everything, even if the wardrobe didn't allow for her shoulder holster.

A grin tugged at her painted lips. Truthfully, she'd have a hard time explaining why Randee Jones—her alias as PrimeRight's newest accountant—brought a gun on her first day, but she'd find a way to keep the weapon close. Just another necessary accommodation in protecting the top secret prototype.

Randee stepped out of her vehicle, hefting the tote onto her shoulder, then reached in, grabbed her steaming vanilla chai latte and trailed behind Steele. She increased her pace, wobbling slightly on her black leather pumps and splashing a little of the coffee on her wrist.

She winced and slowed down, heels clicking against the cement floor. What she'd give for her comfortable combat boots.

Special Agent in Charge Vargas had recruited her for the PrimeRight case, and Randee hoped it was because of her unblemished employment history. After all, she had a box full of awards and accolades as confirmation of her outstanding performance.

A decade ago, Randee soared to the top of her class by exceeding the performance of some of the toughest men she'd ever encountered and risen up the ATF ranks with the goal of being promoted to bureau chief before she turned forty. She'd joined the academy at twenty-nine—

making her one of the oldest recruits with eight years as a Nebraska State Patrol trooper under her belt. A lofty ambition at that time. Nearly impossible now since it left a year to accomplish her dream.

However, there was a greater likelihood Sergio chose her because she was the only member of the team with previous accounting experience. No matter. She'd jumped on the opportunity to pose as PrimeRight's accountant while guarding Project Ghost. But seven months of grueling physical agility training had failed to prepare her for the downside of this mission—the required business formal dress code.

Randee hadn't admitted she'd last worn pantyhose at her academy graduation, and her accounting experience occurred before her trooper days. She'd be dragging terms and procedures out from the recesses of her mind for sure. Sergio had teased her about the eight-to-five schedule. Compared to the extensive overtime she normally worked, the office routine would be a vacation.

The rumble of an engine diverted her attention to the garage entrance. A black utility van approached, morning sunlight beaming off the chrome grill. Randee turned and spotted Steele sauntering toward the door of the adjoining laboratory catwalk. Still oblivious to her and his surroundings.

She increased her speed, her gaze bouncing between the van and Steele. Overreacting would blow her cover— a definite negative on day one.

The vehicle advanced at a normal pace. Randee scurried over to the opposite side of the garage, closing the distance between her and Steele, prepared to intervene.

With a roar, the van sped past her and screeched to a halt, blocking her path to the scientist.

Randee dropped the latte, splashing hot liquid onto

her legs. She bolted ahead, tote bouncing against her hip, and rounded the rear of the vehicle as two hooded men—dressed entirely in black—leaped from the open side door.

She lunged, and her bag slipped off her shoulder, then flopped to the floor. Snagging the closest of the assailants, she caught him off guard. With her hand around his chin she yanked him backward, driving her palm into the back of his head in a classic occipital stun maneuver. The latest training technique worked, and the man slumped to the ground.

Randee's gaze flew to Steele, who was swinging his oversize briefcase at the second attacker, and nearly smacked Randee. She ducked as the assailant latched onto the briefcase, tugging it from Steele's hands.

The hooded man faced her with triumph in his eyes until Randee's foot connected with his knee, hyperextending the appendage.

He screamed and dropped to the ground, clutching his injured leg as the briefcase skidded across the concrete.

Steele reached for the case, but the man lurched upward, tugging Steele down to him. The men rolled on the cement in a flurry of punches and kicks.

Randee scanned the area for her tote, spotting the brown-and-pink print several feet away. An unexpected tackle from behind shoved her down. The attacker ran over her—literally, stomping on her back as he sprinted for the briefcase beside Steele and his adversary.

Randee rolled and swept the attacker's legs out from under him. He bounced against the floor, then growled before delivering a sharp blow to her stomach, knocking the wind out of her.

He drew back his arm, preparing for a second hit. Randee blocked the punch, regaining her momentum, and allowed her training to shift her into autopilot. She wrapped her ankle around the man's leg, inverting herself over him, then drove her fists into his ample gut and jaw. She jumped to her feet, ignoring the pain in her hands, and lunged for her bag.

"Forget it! Let's go!" the driver behind her yelled.

Randee spun to see the wounded men retreating into the van. She spotted the briefcase lying beneath a parked sedan as the screech of tires reverberated in the garage, announcing the men's hasty retreat.

Steele rushed to her side. "Ma'am, are you okay?"

Randee glanced up. "Physically, yes, but this isn't the impression I hoped to make on my first day of work here." Assessing her clothing, she frowned at her ripped skirt and the large run in the left leg of her pantyhose.

"You must be Randee Jones. Our new accountant."

"Yes, sir." She walked past the pool of vanilla latte oozing caramel liquid onto the ground.

"Combat skills aren't part of your job description, but you've got those in spades."

Randee swallowed and shrugged. Great. Now what? She snatched the coffee cup with two fingers and dropped it into the closest trash bin. "Self-defense class at the YMCA," she blurted.

He quirked a dark brow over the rim of his glasses, disbelief in his expression. "Ace Steele. My partner, Fritz Nelson, and I own PrimeRight Laboratories, although I'm technically the senior scientist. Not sure if that means I'm old or at the top of the proverbial career ladder." He held out his hand and gave her a firm handshake. Definitely a positive in her book.

"Nice to meet you, Mr. Steele. Here, let me help." She walked to the briefcase, lifted it and passed it to him. "Wow, do you carry an anvil in there?"

"Ace, please." Mahogany curls peppered with silver

highlights framed his face and strong jaw. The man appeared unfazed by the attack, but reservation in his royal blue irises spoke more. Ace Steele was nothing like she'd expected.

"Since we were attacked, I'm hoping I won't be in trouble for my tardiness this morning?" Randee joked.

"I'd say you have a good reason for the delay. Hopefully, the lab's security cameras caught the license plate." He pointed at a silver camera hanging in the corner.

She'd have Sergio pull the footage immediately. "That was crazy. Are these types of occurrences normal around here?" Randee worked to sound curious while masking her interrogator skills. "Got any idea who those men were?"

Steele frowned. "The beginning of the end."

Ace Steele never planned to be a murderer, but that wouldn't matter if the contracted plans for the ATF's top secret 3-D printer ghost gun and bullets, named Project Ghost, landed in the wrong hands. He would bear the burden of and responsibility for numerous deaths. Every life-stealing, disintegrating bullet forever branding him as a killer.

He led Randee into the PrimeRight Laboratory offices while his mind raced in multiple directions. "You'll want to meet with Yolanda to finish your paperwork," he said in a half-hearted introduction to the office manager.

"Good morning." Yolanda stood and greeted Randee, curiosity etched in her expression at the woman's appearance.

Ace gestured toward the phone on Yolanda's desk. "Police are on their way. We were attacked in the garage. Call me when they arrive. I need to talk to Fritz."

Yolanda's hand flew to her mouth.

"Ma'am, are you sure you're all right?" he asked Randee, studying the pretty brunette. Even with her long, disheveled curls and the disrepair to her clothing, she was stunning.

"I'm fine. Thanks, Mr. Steele."

Her wide doe eyes met his, sending a strange jolt through his chest. Ace spun on his heel and murmured, "I'll be back." Then hurried down the hallway determined to aim his cantankerous mood at his partner.

He never should've agreed to the ATF's conditions, but the increase of illegal ghost guns available to criminals at the touch of a 3-D printer was alarming. Anyone with internet had access to download the specifications for printing the external components. The inner workings had not yet been developed or released. Ace was tasked with inventing an entirely printable gun including disintegrating bullets before the criminals beat him to it. The ATF assured him his efforts would be spearheading legislation regarding printer guns while giving the authorities a head start in protective efforts. Which was a nice way of saying, once he finished his portion, the rest was classified and none of his business.

Randee and Ace could've been killed this morning. Although the extensive security embedded inside the briefcase acted like a portable armory, increasing the weight while protecting Project Ghost's plans and latest—functional but not perfected—prototype. At least the attackers hadn't stolen the briefcase. Small consolation since they'd also gotten away.

Randee Jones was nothing like he'd expected of an accountant. She'd been so composed and confident, fighting back against the assailants. The woman intrigued him.

Once more he considered the petite brunette's amazing combat skills. If the YMCA taught that kind of self-defense, he'd recommend them to everyone he knew. But something in his gut said that wasn't where she'd learned to fight.

If only his sister, Cara, had known how to defend herself. If he'd been braver and responded to her murderer the way he'd done today, she'd be alive. And he wouldn't live smothered under the weight of his mistakes. The familiar cloud of guilt he'd befriended after her death hovered close again.

His life wasn't the only one at risk. Randee had been in danger, too, proving he'd made the biggest mistake of his career by agreeing to Ghost's development. And he intended to fix that immediately.

Agitation building with each step, Ace stormed into Fritz's immaculate suite and blurted, "My office. Now."

His partner flashed his million-dollar smile, phone pressed against his ear, and signaled Ace to give him a minute. Fritz procured contracts for intricate project development, and Ghost was PrimeRight's first government deal. He'd hoped to move the laboratory in that direction permanently. He was probably committing Ace to another wretched top secret, stressful project.

Spinning on his heel, Ace walked to his adjacent office and sank onto his desk chair, head in his hands. "Lord, I never meant for it to happen this way."

Did God listen to murderers? Doubtful. What did it matter, anyway? He'd never be forgiven.

"Who're you talking to?" Fritz flipped on the overhead light and strolled in. The man's modern fashion sense was juxtaposed with Ace's boxy black-rimmed glasses and scraggly hair in desperate need of a trim.

"Shut the door."

"Wow, what's up with you?"

"Well, aside from agreeing to develop a weapon I never wanted to be a part of, I was attacked in the parking garage. If Randee hadn't been there—"

"Who?"

"The new accountant."

"He helped save you?" Fritz grinned.

"*She*, who by the way, possesses exceptional battle skills. Someone's out to steal the briefcase and might end up killing me in the process."

"Maybe it was just a mugging."

"Seriously?" Ace growled, lifting his briefcase onto the desk.

"I mean, there's a huge difference between a mugging and someone trying to murder you."

"This isn't good. I don't feel right about developing the prototype."

"Not this again." Fritz flopped on the chair opposite Ace's desk, bordering on the threat of a file folder avalanche. So much for a paperless system. "You've got to change your perception of this project. You're providing a service benefiting thousands."

"Today proved my fears. If the plans end up in the wrong hands, think of the devastation." Ace leaned forward and met Fritz's annoyed gaze. "Tell them you made a mistake, and the prototype is a flop."

Fritz shook his head, not a hair shifting from its gel-plastered place. "It's a done deal. PrimeRight's reputation is on the line."

"The gun's illegal."

"Nothing contracted and ordered by the government is illegal. Everything regarding Ghost belongs to the ATF. The only difference is your brilliance in eliminating the gun's metal components. Your development gives the ATF a heads-up. What they do with the weapon isn't our problem. And for the record, deadly disintegrating ammunition already exists, so it's not like you're some nefarious scientist trying to overtake the world with an evil invention."

"Frangible ammunition—"

Fritz lifted his hands. "Don't use technical terms on me. Remember, I'm just the PR guy."

"Frangible ammunition is the correct term for disintegrating bullets. It was created for training purposes with the promise of low-impact damage at close range. I'm charged with creating the exact opposite. Disintegrating with high-impact damage at close range." Ace lowered his voice. "If criminals get a hold of Ghost, think of the unspeakable damage they'd possess. The gun's undetectable. If they smuggle it into airports, schools or courtrooms, the carnage will be on me!"

"You're delusional if you don't believe crooks are working on weapons exactly like this right now. We're giving our government an advantage by developing it first. We're protecting the public. You're the best, and you can do this. When it's finished, you'll be a hero."

"As if that matters one iota to me."

"Our employees need this contract. PrimeRight needs the money and recognition." Ace didn't miss the hint of desperation in Fritz's tone and his dramatic sigh.

Ace's plea had fallen on deaf and unwavering ears. They'd had this conversation a hundred different ways and gained no ground. Fritz only spoke in dollar signs.

A long moment passed between them. Would his partner finally surrender? A microscopic portion of hope hovered in Ace's mind.

Fritz planted his expensive black leather shoes on the linoleum floor and rested his hands on his knees. "I didn't want to mention this, but the agreement you signed stipulates if we fail to deliver, the ATF will prosecute us for violating the law. They'll deny any involvement, and they won't pay us."

Ace pushed up from his chair, thrusting the seat back

so fast it slammed against the wall. "What? You never told me any of that. I'd never have agreed to the project!"

"Actually, I did. It's in the contract."

Ace paced around his office. "You tricked me."

Fritz snorted. "Hardly. You signed the same documents I did."

"I trusted you."

"And I trust you to do what's right." His friend's tone deepened and took on a hardness Ace didn't recognize. "Without this contract, PrimeRight will go under, and we'll be forced to lay off all our employees. They'll lose their health insurance." Fritz paused.

His words sank in; Ace was being manipulated by his friend, again. He turned and caught a glimpse of Yolanda and Randee through the small window in his door. The women's timed appearance emphasized PrimeRight's predicament. Yolanda smiled and gave Ace a slight wave, which he returned.

"Diego's treatment is going well," Fritz said, tone softening.

Yolanda's seven-year-old son, Diego, had a myriad of medical issues that had kept him hospitalized most of his young life. As a single parent, she worked hard to provide for them, and her insurance benefits were essential. Dread swarmed Ace. He pinched the bridge of his nose.

"I understand your reservations, but we owe our employees to do everything possible to keep our doors open."

Ace shuffled to his chair, slumped onto the seat and held his head in his hands.

"You're not just my business partner, you're my best friend. Think of all the great things you'll be able to do for women like Cara. By keeping guns away from the criminals, you're saving innocent lives."

Once again, Fritz's precise aim bull's-eyed Ace's guilt right in the jugular.

Frustrated at himself for relenting, Ace studied his friend. Everything about Fritz was etched out of a fashion magazine. Not an out-of-place strand in his perfect haircut framing his blemish-free face. Why had he chosen this man to befriend? Fritz was nothing but trouble, from their childhood antics to this project nightmare. He was also the closest person to a brother Ace had ever known, and their thirty-five-year history spoke for itself.

Ace groaned. "Fine. But for the record, Ghost isn't complete. I need an extension."

"Everything looks great on paper."

"Paper and invention are two different things. Once I've got the prototype completed, I'll let you know."

"How much time are we talking?"

"Weeks. Maybe a month."

Fritz shook his head. "Negative."

"I can't make it come together any faster than I already am. I need to eliminate the bugs."

"Like?"

"The bullets haven't passed testing yet, and the removal of metals like tin or copper for the binding agent to the nylon 6 polymer—"

"Whoa, you're talking way over my head."

Ace sighed. "There's no proof Ghost will sustain firing. My experimental tests explode the frame after the first shot. That's unacceptable."

"I've seen the gun and the bullets. They all work."

"I won't release Ghost until I'm sure it's the best product I can create. Do not rush me."

Fritz held up his hands in mock surrender. "Fine. But the delivery date is scheduled, and we'll celebrate at the anniversary event tomorrow night. I don't want to disappoint. This invention will put us on the map. You're going to be a rich man."

As if he cared about money. "I'll do my best."

"There you go, thinking like the innovator you are." Fritz pushed up from the chair. "Guess I'd better meet this ninja-fighting Randee accountant. And you'll have to give a report to the cops." He moved toward the door, then paused. "Thanks, Ace."

"For what? Giving in to you all the time?"

"For having my back. You're the best." Fritz gave a quick slap to the wall, emphasizing his words, before exiting.

Ace removed the thumb drive from the briefcase, booted up his laptop and inserted the device, pulling up the specs for Ghost.

The gun defied the Undetectable Firearms Act by mere existence because it was developed entirely out of plastic. Even the bullets were made from a specially formulated nonmetallic powder binding agent that disintegrated into tiny fragments upon impact. It was impossible to locate via a metal detector.

Innovative in the ATF's hands.

Mass destruction in the hands of criminals.

TWO

Randee forced patience into her response to Officer Paulson's repetitive questions. Ace's irritated expression reflected his equally tedious conversation with the second cop on the other side of the room. Maybe it was wrong to criticize the officers' methods, but their interview process had lagged to an excruciating level of ridiculous and once more, she repeated her rote replies.

No, she didn't know who the men were.

Yes, she'd defended herself.

No, she didn't know why they were attacked.

Three assailants failed to take the briefcase. Did that speak to their inexperience?

Randee glanced at her watch, anxious to talk to Sergio. The morning's ambush only solidified the need to protect both Project Ghost and the scientist from Titus Malte and his cronies. And that meant Steele might be in more danger than they'd anticipated. "I guess that's all I need for now," Paulson announced. "We'll be in touch if we find anything."

The cops sauntered out the door, and Randee heaved a sigh of relief before excusing herself to the restroom at the far end of the building.

She cringed at her reflection in the mirror, then finger-combed her chestnut curls and attempted to repair her ripped skirt with the safety pin Yolanda had provided. Snatching her cell from her tote, she called Sergio twenty minutes past her check-in time.

"I was about to drive down there and storm the gates. You're late. What's going on?" Sergio barked in greeting.

"Sorry, had to do a report with the local PD." Randee launched into an abbreviated version of the morning's events, concluding with, "I believe the assailants work for Malte. There were no license plates on the van, and the men were masked. Doubtful we'll get any leads."

Sergio dived into command mode. "Ishi will get the security camera tapes."

Given the opportunity, Ishi Haramoto, the ATF's technology expert, could've found the lost city of Atlantis. If there were clues on the footage, she'd uncover it.

Sergio continued, "Zimmer and I will handle protection detail for Steele outside his apartment tonight."

"I'll swing by on my way home."

They disconnected, and Randee exited the restroom. She passed through the double doors separating the smaller lab from the main area and noted the setup.

Floor-to-ceiling windows served as the external walls for the two-story PrimeRight building, filtering in natural light from every direction. The laboratory was centered among the surrounding offices in the restricted access section.

Yolanda glanced up as Randee entered the accounting office. Overflowing file boxes lined the walls and floor, and the modest desk held piles of folders.

"I've tried balancing Barry's job and mine. As you can see—" she gestured toward the massive mounds of paper "—he lacked organizational skills."

The accountant's recent resignation due to his illness

had created the perfect undercover position for Randee. Yolanda's comment opened the topic for discussion.

"What happened to Barry?" Randee busied herself straightening the files before they cascaded off the desk.

"He had many medical issues and an ongoing debilitating disease, but he was such a trouper and a hard worker. The last round of treatments really did him in. He kept to himself a lot. Such a nice man—it was awful to see him miserable. Barry moved to Phoenix to be closer to a specialist there. I saw him just before he was transferred from the University of Nebraska Medical Center."

"Had you visited him often?"

Yolanda shrugged. "My son Diego's in the same hospital, so I'd stop by Barry's room, too." A hitch in her voice captured Randee's attention.

The office manager waved her hand. "Sorry, I'm too emotional for my own good sometimes. Especially when I talk about my baby boy." She chuckled. "Oh, he'd be embarrassed if he heard me call him that. He's almost seven and very mature." She withdrew her cell phone, swiped the screen and passed the device to Randee.

Though she was aware of the child's medical issues, the sight of oxygen tubes trailing from his nose caught her off guard. Nothing dissuaded his sweet smile. So much like his mother's.

"Diego has a rare form of leukemia. A name I can barely pronounce, with expensive and unpredictable treatments. He's a fighter, though."

"I'm so sorry." Randee passed the phone back. "He's handsome, certainly gets his good looks from you."

Yolanda's low ponytail accentuated her high cheekbones. Pride and joy filled her large brown eyes, tainted by a hint of sadness. "He's my everything."

Randee's heart squeezed, and a pause hung between them.

"Are you married? Do you have children?"

And there it was. The words Randee hated most in the getting-to-know-you conversation. She shook her head and steadied her voice before responding. "Not yet." More likely, never. Randee's chance for a family was dwindling, as her mother often reminded her.

Yolanda took the hint. "Forgive me. I'm a talker and too nosy. It's nice to have another woman to connect with. I'll help you get started, then leave you to this treasure trove."

Grateful for the change of subject, Randee attempted to gain additional information. Did Yolanda know anything about the attackers? "Thanks again for the safety pin. I'm not sure it'll save the skirt, but I appreciate it."

"I am so sorry you had to endure that horrible incident this morning."

"Has anything like that ever happened here before?"

"No." The talkative woman grew quiet. "This pile is a good place to begin."

A knock on the open door interrupted the conversation, and Fritz Nelson strolled in wearing a Cheshire grin and an expensive tailor-fitted suit. "Randee, glad to see you're settling in. I apologize again for your awful first encounter with PrimeRight."

"It was an interesting way to start the day," she agreed. "Is the area high crime?"

Fritz shook his head. "No, I'm sure it was an isolated incident. I see Yolanda is getting you acclimated to your new digs." He leaned against the wall, brushing off Randee's question.

"Actually, we were just getting started. Thought I'd show Randee the computer system first," Yolanda said, moving around to the laptop.

Fritz's smile broadened. "Our brilliant Yolanda is a

storehouse of wisdom." He stepped toward her and placed his hand on her shoulder.

The woman glowed from his praise. "I was confessing my lack of accounting experience. I've only done the basics, paying the regular bills and payroll."

"She's too modest. Yolanda keeps this place running smooth as corn silk. Whatever questions you have, she's got answers."

"You're too kind." Yolanda practically beamed. Turning to Randee, she said, "I feel guilty leaving you with such a mess."

Randee grabbed a stack off the desk. "No problem. I'm up for the challenge."

Fritz turned on his heel and headed for the door. "I'll let you ladies work. Welcome to the PrimeRight family, Randee."

"Thank you, Mr. Nelson," Randee responded.

"No mister, just Fritz." He drifted out, whistling, and his pungent cologne lingered in the air.

Randee dived in for more information. "You have a tight community here. Not sure I'll get used to calling the partners by their first names."

Yolanda shrugged. "PrimeRight is a family. Formalities aren't a big deal."

"It's nice. Do Ace and Fritz work a lot of hours, too?"

"They're the perfect pairing. Fritz is the face of Prime-Right, gifted in public relations and negotiations." The woman's voice dripped with admiration. "Ace is the brains of the operation. Quiet. Kind and keeps to himself. But the guy might as well live here. He's single and has no children. A total workaholic." As if sensing the power of her words, Yolanda's cheeks reddened, and she looked away.

The comment stung Randee's heart afresh. She had no relationships outside the ATF, either. Her career was her entire life, and she wondered if it was possible to change that trajectory. Not that it mattered. In her mother's judgmental view, Randee chose selfish ambitions and ridiculous dreams of being promoted to bureau chief over a family.

Randee shook off the thoughts and focused on Yolanda's directions in accessing the accounting system. After an extensive morning of training, she left Randee to excavate the mess.

Within a few hours, she had the hang of the software and was digging through the bank reconciliations and payroll records. Yolanda appeared to have several large transactions marked as bonuses. Not unusual, but interesting the other employees didn't have similar payments.

Yolanda entered, purse in hand. "How's it going?"

Randee glanced up, startled. The clock on her desk read seven o'clock. "The day flew by."

"Everyone except Ace has left. Thought you might need rescuing, and we could walk out together."

The mound of paperwork Randee had delved into was still insurmountable. "Who do I ask for approval to work a little longer?"

"Approved. I have few areas of authority, but I can grant your request." Yolanda placed a Chinese takeout menu on the edge of Randee's desk. "Best place to order from if you decide to get dinner. Number three's my favorite."

"Thanks." Randee lifted the item. She needed to find out when Ace would be leaving.

"By the way, Herman is always willing to escort us to our vehicles after hours." Yolanda gestured toward the elderly gentleman pushing a mop in the hallway. He appeared to be over seventy, though he didn't look frail.

"Good to know," Randee said with a grin.

"Don't let his appearance fool you. He was a marine and a professional boxer."

"Impressive. Guess I've got my work cut out for me."

"Could you use some help?" Yolanda hugged her purse. "Diego sleeps a lot, and I hate going home to an empty house."

Randee's heart tugged at the pain in the young mother's eyes. "If you're willing, absolutely."

"Great!" Yolanda set down her purse. "Let's order food first. I always work better on a full stomach. What sounds good to you?"

"I'll take your advice with the number three."

"Good choice. I'll ask Ace what he'd like. Be back in a sec."

Maybe a little bonding over Chinese would have Yolanda divulging more of her history. Why hadn't she mentioned a husband? Divorced? Widowed? Neither?

Were the bonuses legitimate?

Dread weighed on Randee's shoulders.

Oh Lord, please no. Arresting a desperate single mother for embezzling money to cover her son's medical care would be the worst assignment ever.

Ace lifted the prototype, inhaled and aimed into the firing barrel. *Please work.* He pulled the trigger, releasing the anticipated *pop*.

One down. One to go. The second shot was the doozy. The minor success up to this point became irrelevant when the gun deteriorated on multiple fires. If he failed this time, he'd be facing the 3-D printer for the thirty-third time since taking on Project Ghost.

Ace placed the gun on the table and procrastinated pulling the trigger by strolling around the laboratory. When he couldn't hold off any longer, he took four long sips of his soda and returned to the prototype.

He sucked in a breath and repeated the procedure. The

expected blast emanated, but the cracked frame he held immediately extinguished his gratification.

Test fire thirty-two, failed.

"Fantastic." He slid onto the tall chair beside the table and dropped his head into his hands.

Over thirty blundered attempts. What was he doing wrong? Just as well. He'd never wanted the responsibility of this stupid project, anyway. Fritz would have to let him off the hook if he couldn't get the specifications to work. The ATF would be forced to release him from the obligation. Right?

And PrimeRight would go out of business. Yolanda's boy would lose his health insurance, and the single mom would be unemployed, along with forty-nine other people, including him.

There was no wonderful outcome. Either way, the results and consequences rested on his overburdened and under-talented shoulders.

Even Jesus doesn't come to pity parties. Grandma Steele's words echoed in his head.

"Ugh! Yeah, well, Jesus was smarter than me!" He startled at a knock behind him. Irritated, Ace spun around, facing the intruder, and barked, "What?"

Randee stood in the doorway extending a white take-out bag toward him. "Sorry to interrupt. Our dinner's arrived."

Warmth radiated up his neck. Had she heard his tirade? He shifted his gaze to the clock on the wall, avoiding her eyes—7:45 p.m. "Um. Thanks."

He surveyed his work space, littered with plastic remnants and shattered bullets. She hesitated, and he forced a smile in a pathetic effort to hide his grumpiness. "I promise not to bite."

Randee stepped in, and he shoved aside the prototype blueprints. "Might as well take a break since there's not much more I can do with this hunk of junk." He chucked the broken remnants into his overflowing container labeled *Losers*.

She grinned, drawing attention to her flawless teeth. Braces or blessed with good genetics? "That looks interesting. What are you working on?"

"Meet Ghost. Or rather, its failures."

Randee set the bag on the table, delicious aromas wafting from it. "This is the top secret project?"

"Yep, so remember you're sworn to silence, or men in black may show up and haul you away."

She glanced down and smoothed her torn skirt before crossing her arms over her chest.

Ace gave himself a mental slap for bringing up the subject of the morning's danger. "Sorry, that wasn't—"

"It's okay." Randee's eyes softened with understanding. "What happened wasn't your fault. So, tell me, what's different about this gun other than it looks fake?"

"Everything is plastic and produced from that." He gestured toward the 3-D printer.

"Could anybody create one?"

"Anyone with access to a 3-D printer and my specifications. The difference lies in the fact that Ghost also shoots plastic bullets. Unfortunately, I can't seem to keep them from melting or exploding the frame during multiple firings."

"Is that a problem?"

"Only if you want to shoot more than a single round. Which the prototype agreement with the ATF requires." He groaned and ran a hand through his hair. Saying it out loud made his incompetence more pronounced.

"Perhaps sustenance will increase your creativity."

"There you are. I told Randee she needed to drag you

from your brilliance and join us for dinner." Yolanda swept into the lab, exuding her joy and encouragement.

"Yes, ma'am." Ace lifted the blueprints and cleared off the massive table consuming a large portion of the room. Then he dragged over a few chairs.

Yolanda cleaned the surface with a bleach wipe. "How did today's testing go?"

Randee dished out the food, and the three sat down to eat.

Ace bit and ripped apart his dumpling, taking his frustration out on the meal. "Pathetic."

"It's all part of perfecting the development," Yolanda encouraged.

Ace laughed. "Spoken like a true optimist."

She shrugged. "Sometimes it's hard to see the forest with all the discouraging trees. Or something to that effect."

"Fritz is pushing me to finish before the gala, tomorrow night."

"What's that?" Randee inserted.

Yolanda forked a piece of chicken. "This year is Prime-Right's tenth business anniversary. Fritz has wonderful plans for the event, and we'll secretly celebrate Ace's exceptional invention."

Randee frowned. "But I thought you said the project was confidential."

"It is, but the gala is to commemorate the company. He wanted to have the added behind-the-scenes hoopla for the finished contract." Ace sighed and took another bite. "The way things are going, I doubt that'll happen."

"You'll figure this out. I just know it. Between your revolutionary development and Fritz's brilliant party planning, the gala will be off the chain." Yolanda had a warped sense of his abilities, but her idealism brought something special to the lab.

He'd never describe himself as revolutionary, but Ghost was a game changer. And brilliant wasn't how Ace would refer to Fritz. Smart. Charismatic, for sure. They needed more investors, and completing this project might put them in a favorable place for future government contracts. Of course, that also required a successful completion of the job.

"Good company makes food taste so much better," Yolanda remarked, pulling Ace back to the present.

"Agreed," Randee said, scooping a forkful of rice.

"Honestly, Rocko and I skip dinner a lot." Ace munched on an egg roll. Observing the question in Randee's expression, he explained, "He's my cat."

She grinned. "I sort of pictured you with a Doberman pinscher."

Yolanda sputtered and coughed. "Boy, did she misjudge you."

Ace feigned annoyance. "And what's that supposed to mean?"

"You're not a big-dog sort of guy." Yolanda took a bite.

"I think I'm offended." Ace frowned.

Randee leaned back, quirking an eyebrow, and her lips curved. "Actually, now that you mention it, I can see your point, Yolanda."

Ace crossed his arms over his chest. "You know, if I wanted to be abused, I'd take it from a professional and hang out with Fritz. I'm eating my food alone in the conference room."

Yolanda guffawed. "Aw, don't get your beakers in a bubble. We're only saying you've got more cat tendencies. A loner. Unhindered by others."

Ace chuckled. "I guess that works, although Rocko would go whisker-to-whisker with any Doberman."

"No argument there." Yolanda scooped another portion of sesame chicken from the box.

"What a great name for a brute of a cat," Randee said. "I'd love to have a dog, except I'm never home. Maybe I should consider a cat. Does Rocko do dishes or laundry?"

Ace snorted. "He's very self-sufficient, but I'm afraid he hasn't mastered running the dishwasher."

"Diego would love a pet. Perhaps when he comes home, we'll look into rescuing an animal." Yolanda set her fork down and exhaled.

The past year had taken a toll on the young mother and her son. Fritz had suggested PrimeRight pay her extra bonuses as compensation for covering Barry's job. Ace hadn't disputed the offer. They'd hoped to help relieve some of her financial pressure. She'd never asked for a handout and rarely missed a day of work. The woman was a gem. "How's the little man doing?"

Yolanda's smile didn't reach her eyes. "Doctors say the same, but a mother knows. My boy will be back to his mischievous self soon." She faced Randee. "You should've seen the mess Diego and Mr. Funny Man here created when they swapped all the labels on my canned goods."

"Hey, that was his idea," Ace said defensively.

Yolanda snorted. "I'll be keeping an eye on all of you."

Randee laughed, and the sound was nice. It fit her. Charming and classy. Ace jerked away his gaze, realizing too late that he'd been eyeballing her.

The trio finished their meal, making small talk, and when the last egg roll had been consumed, Ace leaned back. "My stomach's too full for me to keep working."

"Ugh, me, too." Yolanda glanced at her watch. "Besides,

I need to get home and do some laundry, or I'll be in this same outfit tomorrow."

"I doubt I'll be wearing this again. Sewing isn't one of my gifts," Randee said, gesturing to her ripped skirt.

Ace studied her, then averted his eyes. He wasn't Fritz, and romance wasn't his thing. No romance. Ever. "Give me a few seconds to shut down here, and I'll walk out with you."

Within ten minutes, he escorted the ladies from the office into the nearly empty garage. Ace waited until the women had walked to their vehicles before bidding them good-night and moving to his twenty-year-old pickup. A vehicle Fritz teased him about driving. Ace liked the reliable and payment-free truck.

Randee climbed into the tan SUV he'd noticed earlier. Not elaborate but definitely nicer than Yolanda's sensible and inexpensive compact car.

Yolanda was the first to leave. Randee appeared to be making a call. She smiled and waved goodbye.

Ace drove out of the garage and onto the road connecting to the highway.

PrimeRight was located in the country, away from the chaos of downtown Omaha, Nebraska, but close enough to be within the city limits. He flipped on the radio, singing along to an old song that reminded him way too much of his youth and the great times he and Cara had shared before her death.

A boat of a car with a lifted hood sat on the side of the road. Ace slowed, pulled up beside two men standing next to the vehicle, then rolled down his window. "Everything okay?"

The taller man's red Husker T-shirt showed from beneath the accompanying plaid button-up. "Evening." He pointed at the broken-down vehicle. "Got a few gallons of gas on you?"

Ace grinned. "No, but I'd be happy to drive you to a station."

The man's face broke into a wide grin. "Thanks! Name's Jud. Let me talk to my boy, and I'll be right back."

Ace shifted into Park while the men conversed and the kid climbed into the car while Jud tugged on a jacket. A check in Ace's gut had him second-guessing his offer. He shoved down the thought. *Stop being paranoid. People help each other in Nebraska.*

Jud slammed shut the hood, giving Ace a glimpse of the younger individual in the driver's seat. *See, everything is fine.*

Headlights illuminated his rearview mirror, and Ace glanced up. Randee's SUV rumbled toward them.

The man climbed in and closed the door. "Let's get moving."

"No prob—" Ace's words were cut off by the gun aimed in his direction.

"You're going to drive where I tell you. Go!"

THREE

Randee accelerated, desperate to catch up to the fading lights of Ace's pickup. Why had she taken the extra minute to check her voice mail messages?

On a normal day, a broken-down vehicle wouldn't raise her suspicions. Except today had been anything but normal, and as she approached, the driver repositioned the car, strategically blocking the road.

A young man stepped out of the run-down behemoth of a relic and leaned against the driver's door, sporting a challenge on his adolescent face. Had to be one of Titus Malte's militia members. Was the man recruiting kids straight out of high school?

Randee's gaze ricocheted to where Ace's pickup turned north, increasing the distance between them. Worry tightened her chest with each separating second.

She honked and waved her arms for the driver to move. He responded with raised hands in a pitiful attempt at helplessness. Skidding to a stop, Randee rolled down her window. "Get out of the way. Now!"

The young man shrugged and moseyed over to her. "Sorry, car keeps dying."

"Get out of the way!" she repeated.

"Can't, lady, this ol' hunk of junk won't start." The smirk on his face said everything his lying lips withheld.

Randee thrust the transmission into Drive and barreled around the rear of the vehicle, descending into the ditch, then bounding back up on the road.

If the headlights beaming in her rearview mirror were any indicator, the supposed stranded motorist was coming after her.

With the pedal to the floor, Randee's motor roared, but she lost sight of the pickup's taillights as Ace turned again. With one hand on the wheel, she withdrew her gun with the other and continued driving as fast as she could safely go, maintaining visual on the car behind her.

The man made a sudden turn and disappeared. Where did he go?

The sun had already set, and the rural landscape lacked streetlights. Rows of harvest-ready cornfields surrounded her, concealing anything in the distance.

"Where are you?" Randee's whispered question referenced both men.

At last, she spotted tiny red illuminations from the parallel road opposite the river. Since Ace wasn't driving a boat, there had to be a way across the water somewhere close.

Reflectors—on what she hoped was a viable bridge—flickered, beckoning Randee. Without contemplating the possible consequences, she shot over the rickety construction, holding her breath and praying it didn't collapse under the weight of her vehicle.

At last her tires met the road again, and with a sigh of relief, Randee closed the distance between them, flickering her brights.

Ace responded with the glaring red of his brake lights. She veered to miss him. Was he out of his mind? He sped up again, then swerved across the single-lane dirt road. Was he fighting the man inside while driving?

The vehicle straightened and this time, he tapped the brakes. Some kind of silent caution to back off? Too late. Her attention was fixed on the shadowed gun barrel pointed at his head. She'd disregard the warning, though she understood his reasoning.

Randee palmed the steering wheel, frustration oozing through her, but she didn't back off. Malte's men had evolved from the morning's tactics. Apparently, trying to take the briefcase wasn't enough—now they had resorted to felony kidnapping.

The truck fishtailed in an unpredictable dance across the road as Ace increased his speed. In the dim light a flurry of movement occupied the cab.

Blinded by the headlights of an oncoming car, Randee shielded her eyes with her gun-wielding hand.

The kidnapper's partner was barreling straight for her.

She slammed on her brakes and yanked the wheel away from the vehicle. He shot in front of her, spewing rocks at her windshield.

Malte's cronies had done their homework learning this area. She'd give them that, but there was no way they'd get Ace and Ghost. Fueled with a new fury, Randee advanced.

The driver reduced his speed, then centered the car on the single-lane road and continued to slow until they were moving along at a snail's pace.

Randee moved to the right. He did the same. She swerved to the left, and he again blocked her.

"I've had enough of you." Randee accelerated, then angled her bumper against his and gave it a nudge, sending the jalopy into a spin. She revved past the car, catching up to Ace.

His truck continued skidding wildly ahead of her. An

overcorrection resulted in the vehicle's nosedive into the bordering ditch. It caught air and rolled out of control. Randee watched in horror as it tumbled side-over-side, crushing the rows of ripe soybean plants.

After three revolutions, the pickup bounced to a halt on its tires in the open land across from her SUV.

She slowed in a cautious approach, spotting the kidnapper's extended gun. Randee ducked just as a bullet impaled her headrest.

She stayed low using her opened door as a shield, and crept along the side of the SUV, Glock trained on the shooter.

"If you come closer, I'll kill him," the man warned.

Good. Ace was still alive. "Let him go."

"Can't do that." He fired again, hitting the SUV's hood. "That's your last warning. The next one goes in his head."

She contemplated her options. The shooter was slouched in the front seat, preventing a clean shot. "I won't leave without Ace."

The rush of an engine approached, and Randee turned, disgusted to see the jalopy pull up behind her SUV.

"Seems we're at an impasse. My compadre's driving us out of here."

"And why would I let that happen?"

"Because if you don't, I'm gonna kill your friend."

A gunshot sent Randee diving to the ground.

The kidnapper cackled. "Little lady, you're surrounded, so just—" His comment was cut off, and a stillness filled the air.

Randee dropped to a squat, ducked behind her SUV's door with her back to the seat and prepared to fire.

Ace's pickup door creaked open.

She steadied her weapon.

Ace's shoulders emerged as he pushed out the unwanted

passenger. The kidnapper tumbled onto the dirt, unconscious.

Randee barely had a chance to process the scene when a blast behind her sent her twisting around. She returned fire, then hollered, "Your partner's out. Give yourself up, kid."

The muted accomplice appeared to consider his limited choices, then jumped back into his behemoth jalopy and sped off.

Ace ran toward her. "Let's get out of here."

Randee met him and moved to the kidnapper. "Not until the cops arrive." She tugged her blouse sleeve over her hand and snatched the gunman's Ruger from the ground.

Ace trailed behind and gestured at the still-unconscious man. "He's out for the count. Got anything I can restrain him with?"

"Yes, I—" Randee paused. That was close. She'd almost blurted she had handcuffs in her tote. That'd be hard to explain without compromising her undercover status. As it was, she'd be justifying her gun. "Rope!" she exclaimed. "Back of my vehicle, in my toolbox."

"You have a toolbox?" He quirked a brow. Randee gave him a steely gaze, and he shrugged. "Be right back."

Ace returned with the rope and secured the man before dragging him over to Randee's SUV. "Sit here," he said, propping up the kidnapper against the front tire. "There, doesn't he look relaxed?"

She laughed. "Other than his drooping head and hands bound behind his back."

Ace tilted his head and gave a satisfied smile. "Yeah, can't change that, though."

"You're having way too much fun with this."

"After the damage he did, I should do worse."

She studied the handsome scientist, immersed in his navy eyes. "Amazing he didn't break your glasses."

"I turned my head in time so he struck my temple instead."

"May I see?"

Ace leaned down.

Randee gently fingered the developing goose egg. "He got you pretty good."

He winced.

"Sorry about that." What was she doing? She jerked back her hand. "I'll call the police."

Eager to put distance between them, Randee moved to the vehicle. Her driver's-side door was still open, and she ducked inside to withdraw her phone. She dialed 911 and gave a synopsis of the situation. The operator advised her that a unit and rescue were on the way.

Randee disconnected and typed a quick message to Sergio. Major development. Second attempt on Steele. Waiting for PD.

His reply was immediate. Are you both okay?

Yes. Will need cover for my gun.

Go with CHP. Contact as soon as you can.

10-4. Randee reached into her tote and removed the concealed handgun permit, prepared to show it to the officers. She placed her weapon and the permit on her seat, then shut the door and faced Ace.

He stared beyond her. "I've had that pickup since high school. Not sure it's reparable. The rear axle is broken."

Guilt assuaged her. Better a damaged truck than a dead scientist. Ace trekked to retrieve the briefcase and returned, his voice somber. "Think the PD will give me a ride?"

"I'll drive you." Maybe Sergio would dip into the ATF's funds to help pay for the repairs. *Yeah, right.* She leaned against the door. "What happened back there?"

He ran a hand over his head. Something Randee noted he did often when stressed. "The guy looked normal. Said he'd run out of gas. I was trying to be a kind Samaritan."

"For anyone else, it would've been a great gesture. At least I got the make, model and most of the jalopy's license plate."

A groan below beckoned.

"Good evening, sunshine." Randee stepped back.

The kidnapper glared before spewing a few choice words.

"That's no way to talk to a lady," Ace replied. "Say you're sorry."

"Or what?" the man growled.

"How's your headache?" Randee asked.

He clamped his mouth shut.

"Your compadre abandoned you. That can't be a good sign," she pressed.

"Save your breath. I ain't talkin' to neither of you," he groused.

"Doesn't matter, the cops will be here soon. Of course, if I were you, I'd consider talking to them. Give up your partner and you might reduce your own charges." She bit her lip. That sounded too much like cop talk.

Sirens in the distance warned that the police were nearing. Two life-threatening incidents in one day were more than she cared to deal with. Not to mention another belabored conversation with Officer Paulson. But the events were sufficient proof Ace required more than an undercover agent overseeing the project. The man needed a bodyguard.

She'd be both, further complicating her job.

"Thanks again, Gus," Ace said, shaking the man's calloused hand. Gus Yale owned the shop the Steeles had used for as long as he could remember. The guy was ancient but still managed an honest and thriving business.

Gus gave him an affectionate and vigorous slap on the back. "We'll get her taken care of. Give me a call in the morning." He turned and headed to his tow truck.

Ace joined Randee in her SUV and snapped on his seat belt. "Sorry that took so long."

"I'm glad you have someone you trust to do the work. Will he be able to fix the damage?" Randee started the engine and pulled away from the accident site.

"Gus says anything's fixable." He sighed, not wanting to think about how much the repairs would cost. "Do you always carry a gun?" The question escaped Ace's mouth before he realized he'd spoken. Exhaustion apparently brought out his bolder side.

His sister, Cara, would've carried a gun out of fear thanks to her violent, obsessive ex-boyfriend. Prior to his incarceration for stalking, the creep's threats kept Cara and their entire family on edge. Was that Randee's reasoning? If so, who was she afraid of and why?

"Yes." Randee gripped the wheel.

Something told him the weapon-toting accountant didn't possess a fear molecule in her body. Had she once been a CIA agent? He grinned at the silly idea and studied the pretty brunette. She'd experienced every part of his crazy day with her impeccable timing. Randee exuded confidence that complemented her already attractive persona.

Ace averted his gaze. Whoa. Totally inappropriate

thinking. They were coworkers, nothing more. He leaned back in the passenger seat. The weight of the day descended on his shoulders, adding to his exhaustion. And with it, the guilt-tainted memories of his failure to protect Cara.

Randee reminded him so much of his sister. Had it been twenty-five years since her murder? A lifetime ago and yesterday all at the same time. They'd missed out on every great adulthood rite of passage, like her wedding and motherhood. She would've had several amazing kids, and they'd have called him Uncle Ace and...that would never happen. She'd died because of him.

His life wasn't the only one at risk. Randee—an innocent party tossed onto this insane battlefield—was also in danger. How would he protect her?

"If you're determined to continue these deadly situations, we might want to establish a distress signal. Although tapping your brakes was satisfactory."

Ace sighed. "Actually, I did that to throw off the guy. It worked until he clocked me." He rubbed the tender spot. "Then I saw you in the rearview mirror. I'm certain he didn't realize you were following us at first."

"Probably figured his loser partner had caught up. He'd blocked the road with that monstrosity of a car."

"Somehow I'm guessing that didn't faze you."

"Nope." She shrugged.

He considered confessing gratitude that she hadn't backed off. Though he hadn't meant for her to come to his rescue, he'd hoped she'd interpret the warning and call for help. And he hadn't a single clue what to do after that. Ace Michael Steele possessed a doctorate and had the student loans to prove it, but surviving mad kidnappers hadn't been one of his courses.

"I need to talk to Fritz," he mumbled.

"I'd agree. Is he on someone's list, too?"

"Doubtful." Because Fritz wasn't Ghost's developer. No, completing the exasperating project wasn't worth dying for. He couldn't continue dodging maniacs at every turn.

Yet someone wanted Ghost, and it appeared they'd do anything and everything including kidnapping and murder to get it. What would happen if he refused to comply with their demands?

He shivered at the unpleasant consideration. The faster he finished Ghost, the safer everyone would be. But what happened after that? Did the ATF provide protection, or did that fall under the responsibility of another government agency? Perhaps he should've negotiated his future in more specific terms.

"You're awful quiet," Randee said.

"I'm contemplating the stupidity of agreeing to this project."

"Are you thinking of backing out?"

That sounded as bad as quitting. Steeles never quit. "No. I'm committed until the end. I just didn't realize I'd need to have a black belt in karate because I'd be tested daily on my physical abilities." His flippant reply exuded whine over humor.

The delay in Randee's response had him wondering if she agreed. "At least Officer Paulson wasn't as determined to ask us the same questions for thirty minutes straight."

Ace smiled. "Definitely. Turn here." He pointed to the off-ramp from the highway. He continued to guide Randee to his apartment until she pulled up to his building. "This is it, number five."

"This is a nice area. Very quiet."

Six buildings with four units each made up the complex. One-bedrooms with two-bedrooms on either side.

"The complex is older. The managers keep it clean, rent is reasonable and they allow cats." Important requirements for Ace. Fritz forever teased him about wasting money in rent, but Ace preferred the freedom of living unbound by debt. The same reason he drove the old truck.

He sighed. Had driven. He prayed Gus really could fix the damage because Ace hated the thought of having to buy a new vehicle. A thing he dreaded almost as much as his annual dental appointment.

Randee shifted into Park and swiveled to face him. "I hate to ask this, but would you mind if I used your restroom before I go?"

"Oh, sure. I should've offered."

They exited the SUV and approached his building, climbing the three cement steps to his unit. He inserted his key and paused. Randee stayed behind him. Who could blame her? After their adventurous day, she probably assumed he needed twenty-four-hour supervision.

Was there someone in his apartment? He shook off the thought and turned the dead bolt. No. He was fine.

Ace shoved the door wide and stood in the entrance. He flipped the switch, turning on the table lamp beside his sofa and scanned the open-concept main floor, half expecting to see two armed men waiting for him. Instead, embarrassment at the lack of furnishings in his simple home had him apologizing. "Sorry for the bachelor accommodations. Come on in. Bathroom's upstairs." He gestured toward the stairs at the back side of the room.

"Great. Be right back." Randee hurried up the steps.

Ace clutched the albatross of a suitcase and proceeded to turn on every light, highlighting the worn carpet in desperate need of replacement, but he didn't require much. He'd never had visitors, didn't date, and Rocko was low-maintenance.

As if on cue, the black-and-gray tabby sauntered out of the kitchen, meowing his welcome before hopping onto the single couch. Ace lifted him, sending the animal into a rendition of vibrating purrs. "You won't believe the day I've had."

"Thank you," Randee said, descending the stairs. "And this must be Rocko."

Ace smiled and pivoted to provide her a better view. She scratched under the feline's chin, and Rocko responded with lazy, adoring eyes. "I'll swing by in the morning and give you a lift to the office."

He grimaced. "I forgot about that. Sure you wouldn't mind?"

"Not at all. I don't live far from here. It's on my way."

"Thanks, Randee, that'd be great." He set Rocko down and exchanged phone numbers with her.

She moved to the door. "Good night."

Ace nodded, feeling as though he should say more. Fritz would be charming, but exhaustion overrode his desire to be anything other than his boring self.

He stood in the doorway, ensuring Randee's safe departure. The vehicle's headlights bounced off the other buildings as she reversed and drove out of the parking lot.

Ace double-checked the dead bolt and window locks, then carried the briefcase up the stairs, flipping off the lights on his way. He inspected the bathroom, then did the same in the bedroom and closet. "Stop being such a chicken. What would you even do if you found an intruder? Smack him with the briefcase?" he mumbled to no one.

He set the impenetrable case on his bed and applied his fingerprint, then typed in the seven-digit code. The lock released with a *click*. The prototype prints lay inside, along with the thumb drive loaded with every file needed to create Ghost's image. He studied the blueprints again. Where did the malfunctioning component—that exploded the gun into pieces—exist?

Rocko jumped onto the bed and made himself comfortable in the briefcase, sprawling out on the papers. His amber eyes blinked at Acc.

"I take it you're in need of attention?"

The cat yawned.

"Or implying I'm too consumed with this stupid project?" Ace sighed and lifted the cat—meowing his impatience at the intrusion—and closed the briefcase.

Tomorrow he'd find the mistake and complete Ghost, finishing the horrific project once and for all. Dread clung to his shoulders, because after the day he'd endured, he worried tomorrow's danger would be worse.

FOUR

Randee surveyed the two men confined with her in the blacked-out utility van. Was death by asphyxiation their plan?

Thirty minutes holed up with her boss, Sergio Vargas, and her partner, Wesley Zimmer—both waging a silent demonstration war of the worst colognes ever marketed—was more than enough to suffocate her.

When she made bureau chief, she'd enact a scent-free rule for future stakeouts. Randee took a swig of her cola, hoping to wash the taste from her mouth. "You two need to reconsider your fragrance choices." She pressed her sleeve against her wrinkled nose. "Can't we open a door and vent this place?"

"It's ten degrees outside, and you wanna open a window?" Wesley shook his head. "I'm not freezing for anybody." The man's six-foot-five-inch and two-hundred-fifty-pound linebacker body took up more than half the room in the van. He sat legs outstretched with his brown leather wing tip shoes wiggling next to her. Wesley lived to torment her—like an annoying little brother—while stuffing his face and watching her do all the work.

"The disdainful odor you're referring to is Zimmer's. *My* cologne is expensive and tastefully applied," Special

Agent in Charge Sergio Vargas said defensively. "We can't risk any exposure to us. Besides, you're almost done for the evening. Steele's bent on keeping you on your protective toes, so you'd better enjoy your beauty sleep."

Randee chuckled. "This definitely hasn't been the mellow accountant undercover job I pictured." She turned up the laptop speakers and listened as Ace talked to Rocko. A slight twinge of guilt for deceiving the scientist gave her pause. She'd installed an audio bug when she'd asked to use his restroom. Wesley had secured a camera above his front door prior to their arrival. Her team needed the advantage in order to ensure no one broke into his home and to monitor any phone conversations.

"Tomorrow, we'll—"

Randee tuned out the side discussion Wesley and Sergio held as she listened to Ace. "I keep reminding myself that I'm doing this project to prevent anyone else from losing their sister, Rocko."

Ishi's extensive background research on the partners had yielded the devastating story of Cara Steele's brutal murder. The girl's ex-boyfriend—previously incarcerated for stalking—was released early on parole her freshman year of college. He returned to the Steele ranch with an illegally purchased gun when Cara was alone. He shot and killed the girl, then took his own life in a murder-suicide. Fourteen-year-old Ace arrived home shortly before his parents and discovered the bodies.

Randee's instincts said Ace wasn't Malte's spy. The speakers went quiet.

"Sounds like Steele's gone to bed." Sergio's announcement of the obvious redirected Randee's attention. She glanced up as he snatched one of Wesley's fries.

"Uh-uh, y'all weren't hungry when I ordered. Don't be

stealing my food." Wesley moved his grease-soaked meal away from Sergio and Randee.

"No worries about that here. I can't stomach anything over your nasty cologne." She wrinkled her nose.

Wesley feigned hurt, slapping a hand over his heart. "This is no cheap knockoff. It's the real deal. Besides, Larissa says it gives me a manly air."

Randee laughed, grateful to be herself with her team again. "So do sweaty socks, but I wouldn't recommend those, either."

"Ready?" Ishi's soft voice interrupted via Randee's ear piece.

"Yes, ma'am." She addressed the men. "Ishi's playing the earlier call."

Wesley harrumphed and leaned back crossing his legs. "Probably just another—"

"Shh!" She glared, silencing him, then focused on the laptop where she communicated with Ishi via instant messaging.

Ishi had hacked into the PrimeRight system from their main office and traced every call.

Wesley rolled his eyes and took an exaggerated messy bite of his triple-stacked bacon cheeseburger. The man had to have arteries of iron to eat the way he did.

"Is the project complete?" The voice-masked audio came over loud and clear.

Phone signal bounced between cell phone towers and they're using voice-changing software. Impossible to trace. These guys are good, Ishi typed.

"Almost, but there are complications," another voice responded.

Even with the software, the caller's irritation bled through the recording. "Like?"

Hesitation, then the second person said, "I'm not sure, but sounds as if Ghost will be done soon."

Randee responded, Whose phone?

Main floor big laboratory.

They had tapped every line, and relief coursed through Randee. The call hadn't originated from Ace's office. The mole's affiliation with Malte alone would earn him a nice six-by-nine room on a twenty-to-life vacation.

"If you're playing games, I assure you—" the first caller roared.

"I'm not!" The voice alteration did nothing to hide the desperation in the person's tone. "I'm doing what you asked."

A chuckle. "And you'd better continue to cooperate. You're aware of what's at stake."

"Yes." Nearly a whisper. The line went dead.

That's it, Ishi typed.

Randee removed the earpiece and met Wesley's gaze. "Was it just me or does it sound like our spy isn't a willing participant?"

"We came to the same conclusion." Sergio leaned in closer.

"We—and by we, I mean you, Undercover Wonder—" Wesley waggled his eyebrows and continued "—should convince the person to let us help them."

"I'd have to identify him first. And a blackmailed victim is undeterred if the consequences are high enough," Randee said.

"The stakes might range from a family member to a deep dark secret. Is Steele finished with the prototype?" Sergio asked.

"He's achieved the single shot with success, but Ghost shatters during subsequent firing," Randee reported.

"Not good news. I want to wrap up this operation ASAP." Sergio rubbed his temples, his classic sign of worry. "Wait until you hear the next call."

Here it comes, Ishi typed.

Randee inserted the earpiece again.

"What's the update?" the first voice demanded. "Did you get it?"

"Not yet. It's almost finished."

The man snorted. "Keep a close eye on our friend. I'll remind you we have a deal, and your deadline's approaching."

"I know," the caller whispered.

"Once I have the prototype, we will eliminate all liabilities, and you're going to help, or you'll be one of them."

A gasp. "What do you mean?"

"You are stupid, aren't you?"

"But you promised no one would get hurt if I obeyed your demands."

"I changed my mind."

The call ended.

Randee groaned. "I'm taking a shot in the dark here, but sounds like he's talking about Steele. Guess I should anticipate another battle tomorrow. Perhaps moving the scientist somewhere outside of PrimeRight is wiser."

Sergio shook his head. "Negative. I hope Steele isn't our mole, but no one is above suspicion right now. Just keep doing your job, including maintaining your cover."

"With all due respect, sir," Randee said, "we're only monitoring calls. PrimeRight isn't a twenty-four-hour operation, and there are multiple floors. I can't watch everyone at all times. We need video."

"Agreed," Sergio replied. "With the caller moving around, using a different phone each time, the trace is taking too long."

"No coincidence there." Wesley stuffed another fry into his mouth.

"Should have video by morning," Ishi said over the laptop speaker.

"Do you ever sleep?" Randee quipped.

"I'll sleep when I'm dead." Ishi chuckled.

"Is there more happening inside the building with Steele?" Wesley adjusted his position, rocking the van.

"If there is, Randee will find it," Sergio assured.

"Why we gotta sit out here, anyway? The scientist is about as boring as they come. Dude's been snoring up a storm, 'bout to blow out my earpiece." Wesley swirled a fry in ketchup.

"Aren't you full yet? You've been eating nonstop since I got here." Randee's back ached, and her behind had gone numb from sitting on the floor of the van. But she'd never complain out loud.

"I need to keep up my strength," Wesley grumbled.

Randee laughed. "How Larissa puts up with you I'll never understand."

"Once Ishi establishes the connection for the cameras, she'll send it to your cell phone," Sergio interrupted. He swiped at his iPad, glanced up and snatched a fry from Wesley's stash, earning him a glower.

Randee redirected the conversation. "I noticed several high-dollar transactions marked as bonuses to the office manager, Yolanda Ruiz."

"Embezzlement?" Sergio asked.

Randee shook her head. "I don't think so. The woman has a terminally ill child, but neither partner has mentioned issues and both had to sign the checks. To be sure, Ishi, please access Ruiz's bank account and search for anything suspicious."

"On it. Talk to you all later. And Randee, take care of yourself," she said, signing off in their team's usual manner.

"Take care of you," Randee answered, removing the earpiece. "There's a possibility the transactions are legit, but they seem excessive for a company riding above the red. Guess I'd better get going." She paused, hand on the sliding door. "Did you get any information off the garage cameras?"

"None. As you suspected, the vehicle wasn't plated, and the men's disguises covered their faces." Sergio popped another of Wesley's fries in his mouth.

"Don't mind me and my dinner," Wesley complained.

Just to annoy him, Randee snatched a few before gathering up her tote. "I'll leave you two to do your thing." She slipped out of the van and closed the door softly.

Sergio had parked on the corner of Ace's block, where they'd have a clear line of sight and easy access to exit should a pursuit be necessary. She surveyed the area, then, keeping within the shadows, started to make her way back to where she'd parked her SUV when movement got her attention.

Randee ducked behind a parked car, watching as the familiar form of the kidnapper's partner slithered up to Ace's door, knelt and proceeded to pick the lock.

Wow, Malte's cronies had tenacity. She texted Sergio from her vantage point while maintaining visual. Within seconds, he and Wesley descended on the intruder.

For all his bulk, Wesley had the stealth of a panther. He pounced and knocked out the man before he knew what hit him, all without alerting the neighbors. The complex remained quiet, and no lights or sounds appeared from the other apartments. Wesley tossed the man over his burly shoulder in a fireman carry and saluted Randee.

She chuckled and hurried to her SUV. Tension still tightened her shoulders, and her body screamed exhaustion while her brain spun into overdrive.

Malte was nothing if not persistent. The criminals they'd encountered throughout the day proved high standards weren't a requirement for the militia leader's choice of followers. However, he had a plentiful reserve of willing idiots and financial resources.

Randee considered the kidnapping attempt. If Malte had Ace, he'd have the ability to produce an unlimited supply of the prototypes, and his growing impatience motivated him to speed up the process. The militia leader's determination wouldn't stop until he got the prototype. He'd force alterations to Ghost that benefited him, then rid himself of the liability. Randee bristled at the threat to Ace. The kind man was no match for Malte, who'd already ordered the deaths of all those involved, including Randee.

They'd successfully thwarted the criminal's efforts today, but Ace's words from the morning echoed in her mind: *It's the beginning of the end.* And she couldn't agree more.

Rays of early-morning light filtered through the blinds and mingled with the cheerful chirping of birds. "You'll never get them." Ace yawned his comment to Rocko, perched on the windowsill above his bed.

The cat stared out the glass in his daily preparation for attack on one of the unsuspecting feathered singers. Each pass of his swishing tail tickled Ace's nose like a countdown, forcing him out of bed. He swiped the furry appendage away, groaned and rubbed his stiff neck. "I'm up, I'm up."

Rocko meowed and pawed at the glass, undeterred from his bird-acquiring position.

"Give it up." Ace threw his legs over the bed and pushed away the covers. The briefcase—noose, millstone or whatever definition one attributed to a deadly project that created issues of personal safety—sat beside him, safe and secure.

As he did every morning, he opened the case, ensuring the plans remained secure. If only he'd been allowed to copy the files, he wouldn't have to haul the stupid beast back and forth. But the stipulations of the agreement mandated the case be in his possession at all times, and only his fingerprint unlocked the code.

No time to think about that today. Ace secured the items and carried the briefcase into the bathroom, locked the door and showered.

Twenty minutes later, he stood in his kitchen staring at the coffee maker and remembered he was out of groceries and needed to go the store. He owed Randee for being his personal chauffeur. At the very least, he'd offer to treat her to a cup of coffee from one of those fancy places. Since there happened to be one nearby, he'd suggest they stop on the way.

Ace's phone dinged with a text. He didn't restrain the smile creasing his lips.

Be there at 7:30.

Thanks. He added a smiley emoji. Whoever invented the little communication technique was brilliant. What he'd never have the courage to do in person, he achieved via a small yellow face.

The tan SUV pulled up right on time. Randee had to be ex-military, or something equally regimented. Probably an unfair assessment—perhaps other women arrived on time, but Cara and his mother never achieved that goal. Even Yolanda fluttered in ten or fifteen minutes after the hour each day.

"Good morning," Randee greeted him as he entered her vehicle.

The flowery scent of her shampoo wafted to him, and

he had to resist the urge to inhale deeply. "Thanks again for coming to my rescue," he teased half-heartedly, though there was more truth to the comment than he cared to admit. Randee Jones had been rescuing him a lot over the past twenty-four hours. "Did you get a good night's sleep?" He snapped on his seat belt.

"My usual. You?" She put the vehicle into Reverse.

"Someone could've broken into my house, and I'd have slept right through it."

Randee glanced over and a glimmer he couldn't quite explain flickered in her eyes. "Good to hear."

"Mind if we stop for coffee on the way? My treat."

"Music to my caffeine-deficient ears." She drove to the closest coffeehouse, and Ace ordered a boring large black coffee.

"I'll have a double-pump, triple-shot, low-fat, high-foam, extra-hot, peppermint and white chocolate mocha with whipped cream," Randee rattled off into the speaker.

He chuckled. "I used that formula in a college chemistry experiment."

She pulled up to the window and passed his drink to him. "I'm sure I'm one of those people they hate serving, but I like what I like."

A few minutes later, they pulled into the PrimeRight garage, and Ace scanned the area. "I don't see any nefarious black utility vans today."

"Maybe they're using a different vehicle." Randee grinned and gave a one-shoulder shrug.

Her comment, whether teasing or a brush-off, failed to alleviate Ace's apprehension, and he surveyed the garage again. He exited the SUV and didn't relax until they entered PrimeRight.

Fritz stepped into his office, shoulders back, legs stiffly

planted, and pushed up his sleeves wearing his agenda-filled-business-meeting face. "Morning."

"Whatever it is, I'm not interested." Ace shoved open his door and set the briefcase on his desk.

"What?" Fritz slid into the chair, his voice smoother than melting butter. "Wait till I explain."

Ace spun his chair to face the window only to find Fritz's smug reflection in the glass. "No."

"Ace—"

"I'm in the middle of finishing the last idea you roped me into, and in case you haven't noticed, I've had two significant attempts on my life. Which reminds me—" he swiveled around and leaned across the desk "—why are these crazy people singling me out?"

Fritz furrowed his brow and leaned forward. "Two attempts? When did the second happen?"

Ace groaned, brushing back his unruly curls from his face, then launched into the abbreviated explanation from the night before.

"Man, that's a little disturbing."

"No kidding. So I'll ask again, why me?"

Fritz shrugged. "Honestly, I don't know. My guess is that they know I'm the cheery, handsome, talkative member of our duo, and you're the brains."

In other words, Ace was the unattractive nerd. "Thanks a lot."

"I mean, I'm not the developer."

"You have access to everything I do."

"I don't."

Was he hinting? "Do you want to share custody of the briefcase?"

Fritz held up his hands. "Nope. I'm simply clarifying why, of the two of us, you're in these criminals' crosshairs.

Tell you what, I'll contact the ATF person and ask them to ramp up security."

"Yeah, do that."

"However, if sharing the responsibility would alleviate your stress, I'll take it."

Ace shook his head, wrestling with a strange possessiveness over the project.

"Okay...what about leaving the briefcase here at the office or at my house in my personal safe. Al Capone wouldn't have been able to break into that."

Hesitation at the idea of abandoning the albatross struck Ace. Did he want to share his brainchild? The strange conflict of emotions gave him pause. "That's not a bad idea, but it's a topic to broach with the ATF."

"I'll ask when I call. Now that we resolved your issue..."

"No. For the last time, whatever it is, no. If you'll excuse me, I've got an idea to revise the test."

"Great. I want to see this bad boy come to life." His partner ignored the obvious dismissal.

Ace sighed. "Swing by the lab later."

"Everything is coming together nicely for tonight's gala."

Another reminder that the clock was ticking on this project. Ace's lack of facial expression control had Fritz lifting his hands in mock surrender. "No pressure, just keeping you updated."

"I may need a ride this evening if Gus can't fix my pickup. Which reminds me, I should call him this morning. Thankfully, he towed it back to his shop last night."

Fritz chuckled. "I can't believe that guy's still in business. You deserve a new vehicle. Let's take the afternoon off and go car shopping."

"No, thanks." Fritz loved any excuse not to work, but Ace didn't have time for that today.

"Your reluctance wouldn't be a result of our new accountant providing you daily transportation, would it?" Fritz waggled his eyebrows.

Ace rolled his eyes, ignoring the warmth emanating up his neck. "Gus said the truck repairs are manageable."

"Hmm. If you say so," Fritz laughed. "I'll swing by the lab around lunchtime so you can show off your progress on Ghost." He stood and slapped the door frame in his usual mode of departure. "By the way, don't forget your monkey suit for tonight."

"Yes, Mother, it's hanging in my closet."

Fritz's chuckle echoed in the hallway. His partner—polar opposite to Ace in every way—had an indisputable way of lightening the atmosphere.

The day passed in a blur and by noon, Ace's frustration reached a new level of discouragement, sucking the creative energy from his brain.

He took a long swig of his Dr Pepper. There was no way he'd have Ghost finished in time for the gala tonight. He needed to replenish his supplies, and at the rate he was botching the project, he might need them in bulk. Stubbornness reared its ugly head, reminding him defeat wasn't an option. Not when he was so close he smelled victory.

Fritz appeared at the door of the laboratory. "Ready to demonstrate your genius?"

Ace gestured to the table. "The prototype is almost finished printing. Grab a seat and put on the safety equipment."

Fritz inserted the earplugs, placed the headset over his ears and slipped on the clear glasses. Ace checked the 3-D printer, removed test number forty, and donned his own safety equipment.

He loaded the bullets into the magazine, said a quick prayer, then with a steady hand, aimed and fired.

"Outstanding!" Fritz jumped to his feet.

Ace bit back the sarcastic retort. His partner had no clue how this worked. "The first fire isn't the issue."

"Oh." Fritz sat down again with a sheepish expression and motioned for Ace to continue.

Once more, he aimed and fired. The gun held. "Yes!" It worked. The latest adjustment worked! But the third shot would be the most telling. Fritz remained silent, expectancy oozing from him. Ace held his breath and released the last round.

The gun fractured into pieces. Any remnants of hope evaporated. Too frustrated to even demonstrate his discouragement, he tossed the gun into the *loser* pile.

"Two successful firings." Fritz slapped him on the back. "I say we tell the ATF it's a success."

Ace spun around. "Two isn't enough."

"It's sufficient for the Feds."

"It's not acceptable!"

Fritz appeared taken aback. Good. He needed to stop rushing the process. Stop pushing Ace to deliver a half-completed project. "I'll let you know when Ghost is ready."

Fritz removed his safety equipment. "Ace, take a break. Work on the project after the event tonight. I'll talk to the ATF and ask for an extension."

Ace paused and studied his friend. Why the sudden change? "You'd do that?" Not that it mattered; there wasn't a way to force everything to come together.

"Absolutely. I'm worried about you. You're going to stroke out. And I feel guilty."

"You don't possess the emotion."

Fritz smirked. "Can't help but wonder if I'm adding pressure and hindering your progress with the project."

"It's certainly not helping."

Fritz winced and slid into the chair opposite Ace. "I'm

sorry, man. The truth is, I'm worried about our finances here. We need this contract."

"I know." Ace's cell phone rang, providing a well-timed interruption.

"Hey, Ace, this is Gus. We were able to get your pickup running again. It's not pretty, though. You did a number on it."

Ace grimaced. "Yeah."

"Smitty will drop it off in about an hour."

"Perfect, thank you." He hung up and faced Fritz. "My transportation problem's solved. Gus fixed my truck."

Fritz shrugged and headed for the door. "Bummer. No more carpooling with Randee."

"Whatever." He waved off his friend and assembled a new test.

But as the day wore on, no matter how hard he tried, Ace couldn't shake the twinge of disappointment. He had enjoyed the extra time and excuse to be with Randee. She was easy to talk to, attractive and smart.

Palming the next test prototype, Ace prepared to fire. Three successful firings would constitute a success. *Please work. Please work.* The mantra had become as natural as breathing. He aimed and released the third round. The gun held!

"Yes!" Ace did a fist pump.

"Good news?" Randee entered the lab carrying a stack of folders.

Without thinking, he rushed to her and lifted her in a hug. "It worked!" Suddenly very aware of his faux pas, he set her down. "Sorry." The thrill of the moment overrode his embarrassment. "I got three consecutive rounds fired."

"That's fantastic." Her sincere smile warmed him, and he had the incredible urge to hug her again. Instead, he shoved his hands into his lab jacket pockets and stepped back. She must've sensed his awkwardness because she said, "I didn't mean to interrupt. Just wondered if you need a ride home today?"

Randee's thoughtfulness and the ease he felt around her were foreign and exciting. When had he become so aware and cognizant of her presence? The quizzical expression she wore prodded him to respond. "Actually, no. Thanks. Smitty dropped off my pickup earlier, so I should be good to go. The body damage remains, but it runs. Works for me." He was rambling. *Ugh.*

Ace scrubbed a hand over his hair. What was wrong with him? He needed space away from her. Like now. A confusing combination of emotions—somewhere between exasperation and irritability—spurred his next words. "I need to get back to work." He lifted the prototype and prepared to fire.

"Okay." She turned and exited the lab, and her absence registered.

"Off-limits," he murmured to himself.

"Did you say something?" Randee poked her head in again.

Go away. "Sorry, talking to myself."

She grinned. "I do it all the time. I almost forgot, I have a question about a payment that was made—"

Ace turned his back to her. "Sorry, you'll have to talk to Fritz about financial matters." His impatient reply did the job, and Randee's footsteps faded behind him.

Effective immediately he'd enforce a stricter distance from Randee, because she was awakening a vulnerability he couldn't risk right now.

Or ever.

FIVE

The hunt for Malte needed to end tonight.

Ishi advised that there had been increased activity on the phone lines between Malte and his spy during business hours, but she still hadn't succeeded in pinpointing the location or caller. Malte had alluded to his appearance at the gala. At this moment, Randee's team was preparing for the takedown.

Though several employees had made calls using the laboratory landlines, until Ishi deciphered which caller was the spy, they couldn't act on what might be normal business interactions. Fritz Nelson remained at the top of Randee's suspect list. Something about the guy just sat wrong with her.

She studied the text from Sergio again. Keep suspects in view and your eyes wide open.

She groaned. Short of hovering over them or holding everyone hostage, what more could she do? She'd already found a million ridiculous reasons to roam the halls spying on each person's whereabouts. Now only she, Ace and Yolanda remained in the ghost town of a building since everyone had left early to get ready for the gala.

She'd hoped to drive Ace home, ensuring his safety, but his vehicle's repairs had nixed that idea. He was a complicated and unpredictable man. She recalled his spontaneous hug after the successful prototype trial. For the briefest moment, Randee remembered how wonderful it felt to be held.

Fortunately, his about-face icy reception at her accounting inquiries had squelched any misplaced feelings. Not to mention, the rest of the afternoon, he'd dodged her at every turn. Even to the point of pivoting in the hallway when he saw her and scurrying off in the opposite direction. His standoffishness shouted "keep your distance," and the sudden change in his behavior confused her. If Ghost was a success, why was he acting so strange?

Randee stared out the window, realization tackling her with the weight of a sumo wrestler. If Ace was the mole, his sudden shift was easily explained. Exaltation at completing Ghost warred with Malte's demands to hand over the prototype and eliminate all those involved.

She dropped onto her chair, disappointment rushing through her. No. Ace couldn't be working for Malte. But his demeanor said otherwise.

"Ready to go?"

Randee startled and swiveled around.

Ace stood in her office doorway, briefcase in hand. What was up with this guy? He'd gone from avoiding her like she was plague-afflicted to standing at her door. As if sensing her confusion, he explained, "We're the last two in the office."

Okay… "Oh, right. I lost track of the time." She gathered her tote and followed him out, turning off the lights.

Ace moved ahead of her, eliminating the possibility of conversation. Back to avoidance. "Good night, Herman."

The older gentleman glanced up from his diligent mopping. "Evening, Ace. Ms. Jones."

Randee paused. "Will you be joining us at the gala?"

"No, ma'am, my party days are over." The older gentleman chuckled and whispered, "But save me a piece of
cake, would ya?"

"Absolutely. See you tomorrow." She smiled and hurried
to catch up to Ace standing beside the outer doors. Was
Herman the mole? It seemed ludicrous but viable. She'd
contact Ishi as soon as she got into her car.

Randee's scattered thoughts bounced around her brain
as chaotic as kindergartners on an Easter egg hunt. She
was so distracted that when they reached the empty parking garage, she nearly ran into Ace's back. He was a foot
taller than her, so she had to peer around him to see what
had stilled him. Her gaze traveled across the garage and
landed on his aged, dented pickup with four flat tires.

"Are you kidding me?" He reached his vehicle in two
long strides and surveyed the damage. He completed two
full rotations before slamming his hand on the bed.

"I'm guessing they didn't drop it off in that condition?"
Randee asked, hoping to lighten the mood.

His eyes narrowed. "This is ridiculous! Why would
someone slash my tires?"

Randee scanned the garage, lifting her tote higher to
grab her gun. The perpetrator wanted to prevent Ace from
leaving the lab or at least slow him down. Urgency had her
reaching for his arm, but he jerked free, jaw taut. "I'm so
sick and tired of this."

"I understand, but Ace, we'd better get out of here." She
spotted shards of plastic and glass on the ground where
the security cameras had hung that morning.

The sun sat lower in the sky, but it was still early in the
evening. She took out her phone and shot a text to Sergio.
Ace's truck vandalized. Driving him home. Camera's out.

His response came immediately. Headed to his apt now.
Will keep watch.

All she had to do was get Ace safely home. Her team would provide security while she changed, and then she'd pick him up and head to the gala. Easy enough, right? "I'll give you a lift, and we can call the police on the way."

Ace met her gaze and gave a slight shake of his head. "I'll wait for the cops."

They needed to get away from the lab. "I don't mind." The words wouldn't alleviate his irritation, but hopefully they refocused his energy.

"Fine. Thanks." He stomped over to her vehicle and his broad shoulders slumped with what Randee guessed was the weight of his world.

Ace wasn't the mole, but he remained in danger. With Ghost's successful triple round and the apprehension of Malte tonight, they'd close the case and move Ace into protective custody.

Randee wasted no time starting the engine and driving out of the enclosed space. She sped down the county road, her heart pounding. The two miles of county roads before she reached the highway added to her anxiety. Maybe she was overreacting, but everything within her ensured her gut wasn't wrong.

Ace lifted his cell and placed a quick call to the police, advising them of the vehicle vandalism. He slid his phone into his pocket and sighed. "Omaha PD will send an officer over, but when I told them the cameras were broken, they said not to get my hopes up about finding the criminals."

She could've told him that, but having a third party relate bad news to him seemed necessary. "That stinks."

"I live a very boring life. I wear bland colors. I make every effort to blend into the background, and in the last forty-eight hours I've spoken to the police more than..." He turned and faced the passenger window.

Randee glanced at him. Was he thinking of his sister?

"I'm sorry." *Sorry you endured that awful experience and that Malte's torment has no end.*

"Can't last forever, right?" he grunted.

Not if I can help it. "They'll catch the guys. Congratulations, again, on getting Ghost to hold through the third firing."

Her comment worked to redirect his attention, and he brightened slightly. "Thanks."

Uneasiness fell over Randee. Why would Malte slash Ace's tires and then allow them to leave? She made another turn, the highway within sight. The roar of an engine brought the answer.

A pickup approached far too fast, then sped next to her door. Randee let off the gas, allowing the vehicle to pass. But the driver slammed his truck into her door.

She clutched the steering wheel and fought to regain control. "He's trying to run us off the road!"

A second crash had Randee driving into the ditch and nearly hitting a delineator post. She veered around the object and barreled back onto the road.

Ahead, a semi hauling cattle forced her to slow down. They approached a hill with a no-passing zone. She slammed her hands on the steering wheel.

The pursuer accelerated.

"That guy gets any closer and he'll be riding in my back seat."

Ace was already dialing 911, and his voice was remarkably steady as he reported the make and model of the vehicle. He twisted around and took pictures of the car, though the illegally tinted windows prevented them from seeing the driver.

At last they crested the hill and using the decline's momentum, Randee passed the cattle hauler with the pursuer sticking close to her bumper.

The highway was within sight, but Randee's heart dropped at the large detour sign centered across the on-ramp, impeding her from entering.

"Since when is the highway closed?" Ace grumbled.

"Exactly."

Randee's gaze bounced between the truck on her tail and the on-ramp. The detour was a ruse to keep her from exiting the road.

She hoped.

A blast followed by the shattering glass of her rear window had Randee ducking. "Get down!"

Ace slid down in his seat.

The truck's passenger leaned out and aimed again. Randee accelerated, ignoring the detour, and veered around it, merging onto the highway. The passenger fired two more rounds. Shots pinged off her SUV.

She cleared the sign by inches. The truck didn't have enough room to follow, and Randee sped away.

"Is this ever going to end?" Ace barked.

Randee longed to tell him yes, but not for a little while longer. First she had to drop him off at home to get ready for the gala. They had to stick with the plan. In the meantime, she needed to ensure they'd lost the truck. A second on-ramp a mile down the road would provide a way for the truck to trail them.

"Is there an alternate route to your apartment?"

"Yes, we can go through Gretna. It'll make a big loop, but if they're following us, we should be able to lose them."

Once they got to his apartment, Ace would be safe. Sergio would conduct security and follow them to the gala.

The detour, though long, worked at losing Malte's men. Finally, Randee pulled up to Ace's apartment. She spotted the ATF undercover van parked around the corner. "I won't take long to get ready. How about if I return in an hour to pick you up for the gala?"

"Sure. Thanks." Ace shoved open the door, paused and faced her. "I'm sorry, Randee, I don't mean to be rude. I just don't know how to process all of this."

"I'm sure it'll be over soon." And that was one promise she intended to keep. Tonight.

If Marilyn Jareau saw her daughter, she might forgive Randee for joining the ATF. At least until her mother discovered the real reason she was dressed to kill.

Randee smoothed the sequined aqua fabric over her hips and allowed the contouring evening gown to fall in cascading waves to her feet, conveniently concealing her holster and Glock. She gave one final adjustment, ensuring the weapon rested securely against her inner thigh just above her knee. Accessible at a moment's notice and ready for use. With one final perusal, confirming the ensemble worked, she gathered her beaded clutch and called Sergio. "Ready."

"All right, remove the jewelry from the box, and you should be live," Sergio instructed.

Randee opened the case and lifted her final adornment, rhinestone earrings—camouflaging her earpiece and microphone—and matching drop necklace, doubling as a camera.

"Nice, Randee," Wesley boomed in her ear. For all his shortcomings, the man had established himself as the best partner she'd ever had. He was a tad arrogant at times, but that was overshadowed by his wittiness.

"Um, thanks?" She was suddenly conscientious of every move she'd made up to that point.

"We've got visual, and the mic is picking up clearly. Wesley is posing as your limo driver and should be pulling around in the limo Fritz ordered. He'll change at the party, so we'll be dressed as caterers there. As soon as we spot Malte or anyone suspicious, we'll give the signal," Sergio explained for the hundredth time, a normal annoyance from his stress management during any operation.

"Affirmative." Randee adjusted her earring. "Ace is aware the limo is picking us up, correct?"

Sergio chuckled. "Yeah, and based on his heated phone conversation with Fritz, he's not happy about it."

"Tell her about the fit he threw," Wesley inserted.

"Suffice it to say Steele isn't big on the pretentiousness his partner prefers," Sergio replied.

"That's not hard for me to believe. He appears to be down-to-earth." Randee stood before her mirrored bathroom doors, which reflected an image she almost didn't recognize. She'd swept her long brown tresses into an elegant twist with tendrils carefully set free to frame her face. Her blue eyes—too large in her own opinion—stared back beneath the smoky makeup. Something was missing... lipstick. Randee opened her clutch and removed the tube. Two swipes and she popped her lips together. "Good deal. Ready to do some business."

On our way in the limo Fritz ordered, Randee texted Ace.

Will be watching for you. He responded with an eye-rolling emoji.

Flipping off the lights, she made her way to the front door where Wesley waited, sporting a spiffy black suit and tie.

"I wouldn't have recognized you."

He smiled unabashedly and tugged on his lapels. "I look good. You can say it."

She laughed. "You look good."

"Tell me something I don't know."

She tucked her arm in the crook of his and walked to the limo. "Is Larissa okay with this?" Wesley's wife understood acting was a job requirement, but she never wanted to make the woman feel as if she were intruding on the relationship.

"Are you kidding? She picked out the suit." Wesley winked, his brown eyes creased in the corners.

"She's got great taste."

"Naturally, she chose me." He opened the rear door and stepped to the side.

"Wow, we're traveling in style," she murmured, ducking into the elaborate car.

"You deserve it." Wesley closed the door and made his way around to the driver's side. He slid into the seat and shifted into Drive. "Steele should be watching for us."

Randee moved to the rear-facing seat behind him. "I figured you'd pick him up first."

"Nah, your place is on the way. Sergio is keeping watch until we get there."

"Has Ishi identified the caller yet?"

"No, but she will. If Malte's dumb enough to show his ugly mug tonight, we'll be waiting."

"I'm ready to go back to normal."

"We'll have this mission wrapped up in twenty minutes. Just hope I get to eat something first. Booking takes forever." Wesley's stomach rumbled so loudly Randee heard it in the back seat.

"Didn't you inhale a pound of beef already?" She hadn't dared to consume food before stuffing herself into her dress. Her stomach was twisted like a pretzel, preventing her from keeping anything down, anyway.

"He's always eating," Sergio chimed in her earpiece.

She grinned.

"Y'all know I have to eat every two hours to keep up my blood sugar," Wesley argued.

"Like a baby," Sergio commented.

Wesley harrumphed.

"I'll buy you a burger when this is done," Randee promised.

Wesley sat up straighter in the seat. "See, now that's a motivational incentive, boss."

The sight of Ace's apartment squelched Randee's snicker, replacing it with a sudden onset of nervousness. She flexed her hand and sat up straighter, trying to shake off the jitters.

Wesley exited the limo, then moved around to the rear passenger side and opened the door. "Good evening, Mr. Steele."

"Thanks." Ace slid next to her, dragging the always-present briefcase. If her instincts were right, he did a double take. "Wow, you're…beautiful."

Randee's ears warmed, and she glanced down, smoothing her dress with her sweaty palms. "Thank you." She caught a glimpse of Wesley's smirk in the rearview mirror before he raised the window separating the car.

"The limousine was a very nice gesture of Fritz," Randee commented.

"Yeah, he said it was the least he could do after all we've endured the past two days. Personally, I think he just didn't want me showing up in my dented pickup."

Randee chuckled. Or it was a great way to keep them under his thumb. "I've never ridden in a limo before."

"Me either." Ace cleared his throat. "Hey, Randee, I need to apologize."

"For what?"

"My attitude earlier."

"It's totally understandable."

"It's not, but you're kind to extend me grace."

Grace. One word Randee rarely heard since her father's passing and a benefit that had been granted to her even less. "You've been through the wringer. Anyone would be edgy in your situation."

"I guess." He fidgeted with the briefcase handle.

They rode in silence the rest of the commute as the car wove through the streets of downtown Omaha. Streetlamps and neon signs illuminated the city, giving it almost a daylight aura.

Randee leaned back, enjoying the ride.

Wesley rolled down the internal window. "We'll be arriving at the Nelson estate in five minutes."

"Thank you," Ace said, shifting closer to the door as if he couldn't wait to escape the car.

At last they approached the extravagant mansion. Yellow light beamed from the cathedral-style windows, and a long driveway circled to the double doors atop tall slate steps. The mixture of stone and wood provided a combination of modern and classic style to the exterior. Fuchsia and turquoise lights sparkled in the bubbling water fountain centered in the driveway. The only things missing were the red carpet and paparazzi.

Massive wooden doors stood open with two men assisting the guests as they glided up the long staircase.

Randee feigned boredom at the scene, but her insides quaked with curiosity. She glanced down at her own dress, wondering if she'd chosen something too simple for the event.

"You're breathtaking," Ace assured her with a smile.

"I look better, though," Wesley teased in her earpiece.

A light breeze fluttered along her bare shoulders, and she inhaled deeply.

"Shall we?" Ace crooked one arm for her while holding the briefcase in the other, and they headed toward the entry.

The first butler with his overgrown eyebrows and neatly groomed white hair raised his iPad. "Name?"

Fritz appeared from behind the butler and pushed him aside. "Ace, you clean up good, and Randee, you're absolutely stunning."

Ace's hold tightened, and she smiled. "Thank you."

Determined not to teeter unattractively on her stilettos, she focused on taking slow, purposeful steps. The party was in full swing, and people mingled in the beautiful living room. Flames crackled in the oversize fireplace, and instrumental music fluttered from hidden speakers above.

Out of the corner of her eye, Sergio—dressed in a caterer's uniform—lingered with a platter. He met her gaze with an almost imperceptible nod. Relief at her surrounding team members eased the tension in her shoulders.

"Randee, make yourself at home. Ace, I must steal you away for a moment."

Ace released his hold and gripped the briefcase. "Now? We just got here."

"I need to speak with you," Fritz urged, ushering Ace toward the hallway.

He gave Randee one last apologetic frown and traipsed after his partner. Yolanda rushed toward her in a stunning full-length crimson gown. "Isn't this fun? It's like prom night all over again."

That particular connotation did nothing for Randee, but Yolanda didn't need to know why. "You look gorgeous," she said.

Yolanda smiled shyly and grabbed Randee's hand. "I think that describes you, not me. But thank you, anyway." She led the way through the room, introducing Randee to the partygoers with confidence and charm.

Time to roam. The bug hidden in her clutch needed to be planted in the home office before the end of the evening. Yolanda remained at her side, making surreptitious maneuvers difficult.

Fritz and Ace returned, the tension between them palpable. The briefcase no longer swung from Ace's hand. Was that the reason apprehension was written on his face? He stood awkwardly beside his partner, looking uncomfortable and incredibly handsome in his black tux.

Randee absorbed the ambiance of the home decorated in early nouveau riche. Though she knew Fritz came from money, the man had done well in investments, blooming from laboratory rat tycoon into a billionaire. At least before the most recent decline in their finances, which Randee surmised was a result of Fritz's need to maintain his lifestyle. The juxtaposition with Ace's simpler ways wasn't lost on her. They were opposites in every aspect.

Wesley worked the other end of the room, having changed into a white catering uniform complete with a serving tray. He glanced around wearing a mischievous grin and lifted one of the offerings, biting into a pink-and-white flowery concoction. His pinched expression said he didn't enjoy the morsel. She giggled, eliciting Yolanda's quizzical frown.

"Sorry. I do that when I'm nervous," Randee said. The comment wasn't a lie. She felt out of place and vulnerable in the fancy clothing.

Ace's lingering gaze on Randee kept her stomach dancing. A man she didn't recognize entered the home, and Yolanda touched her arm. "I see someone I need to speak with. Would you excuse me a moment?"

"Sure."

Yolanda greeted the stranger with a strained smile.

"Six o'clock," Randee said, taking a glass of ice water from Sergio's platter.

"On it."

"What on earth is that?" Wesley whispered, examining a decorated cracker.

"Caviar," Sergio replied.

"As in fish eggs," Randee said before sipping the water.

Wesley nearly spewed the half-eaten food across the room, but managed to cover with a napkin.

"Smooth," Randee crooned.

"Man, you'd think rich folks would find better things to eat than the innards of some fish." Wesley snatched a cheese-and-cracker combo off another server's outstretched platter.

"Stick with what you know," Sergio advised, moving to the far end of the room where Ace and Fritz leaned against a wall.

Ace met her gaze, smirked and rolled his eyes, conveying his boredom and disinterest in the party. Their unspoken communication was interrupted by Fritz dragging Ace toward a group of women. He slung an arm over Ace's shoulders and by the man's animated gestures and grins, he was introducing Ace to an attractive blonde. A twinge of jealousy coursed through Randee, and she looked away, searching for Yolanda. But the woman was nowhere to be found.

Wesley moved beside her and held out a tray. "For the record, I don't think he's interested in her."

"What?" Randee glanced at Ace and back at her partner. "I don't know what you're talking about."

"Right."

Sergio chimed in, "Just remember, you're still undercover until we get the spy."

Randee rolled her eyes, but the comment acted like a reset button to her brain. Sergio was right; no one was above suspicion, and if they'd read her that easily, she needed to adjust her attitude back to that of an agent. "Hey, where's Yolanda?" she asked, changing the topic.

Wesley jerked his head toward the hallway. "She walked that way with the dude. They looked pretty cozy." He waggled his eyebrows.

"Why didn't you follow her?" Annoyance coursed through Randee as she ducked into the hallway. "Never mind."

"She didn't look like she was bothered by him," he said defensively.

The home office was at the far end of the home near the veranda. Was that where Yolanda was headed? Two women exited the bathroom door to her left, startling Randee.

They ignored her, but the reminder to slow down before drawing unnecessary attention to herself had Randee shifting to a calm glide. Her heart pounded in synchronization with her heels clicking on the stone tiles. When she reached the veranda's French doors, she paused and shifted closer to the wall.

Two figures—Yolanda and the stranger—appeared to be engaged in a contentious discussion. Their distance and the burbling fountain in the center of the elaborate lanai hindered Randee from eavesdropping. Yolanda made wide gestures with her arms, clearly agitated.

Randee prepared to intervene.

Yolanda jerked free and stormed several steps before the stranger reached her. He leaned in and whispered something in her ear. Yolanda's countenance calmed. She nodded and took his hand and they walked back in Randee's direction.

Randee spun on her heel and scurried around the corner into the hallway, aiming for the home office door. She glanced over her shoulder, confirming no one saw her, and slipped through one of the double wooden doors, turned and gasped.

SIX

Randee's unexpected intrusion had Ace jerking upright so fast, a blast of nerve pain radiated down his neck.

"Are you hiding out, or did I interrupt you in the middle of a heist?" She gestured toward the safe.

"I'm not that adventurous." *Or courageous.* He leaned against the wall and massaged the afflicted area. Hadn't he locked the door?

"Guess this isn't the ladies' room," Randee said with a shrug.

He admired the way her sequined evening gown transformed her natural beauty into elegance. She lifted a perfectly sculpted eyebrow, reminding him he'd stared a second too long.

Ace cleared his throat, providing a momentary distraction, but his pulse quickened in her presence regardless. Ducking to concentrate on the safe, he pointed at the adjacent door and mumbled, "The office has a private bathroom."

Either she didn't notice his awkwardness, or she was gracious enough to ignore it, because she moved toward him, her gown swaying softly with each step. "I wondered where Fritz had dragged you off earlier. I'm guessing he encouraged you to leave the briefcase in the safe?"

"As much as I detest carrying the stupid thing, it was a

strange reprieve." For a moment, he relished that Randee had noticed his absence. The thought pleased him, and he quickly avoided her eyes by turning his back and withdrawing the case.

Fritz had pulled him into the office bursting with excitement about his big surprise for the guests, but he'd refused to share any details. In his conspiratorial tone, he'd guaranteed the night would be memorable. Fritz had coaxed him to relax and park Ghost in the safe while encouraging him to mingle with the single women. After a brief discussion, Fritz won—as always—and Ace had locked the briefcase in the office.

He shut the safe's camouflaged door—a large tacky landscape picture—then walked over and dropped onto a wingback chair. "Are you enjoying the party?"

"It's a delightful event. The venue and food are exquisite."

"Fritz loves extravagance. He was a show-off even as a kid."

"I cannot fathom having the amount of money it takes to pay for a home this beautiful."

"It's easy when you're a trust fund baby." Heat rose in his face and he rambled on, "No offense. He can't help being well-to-do."

She paused and tilted her head, lips curved upward. "It sure makes for an easier start. My first apartment was a run-down studio with built-in cockroaches on the bad side of town. I didn't mind, though—I was thrilled to be out on my own until I learned cockroaches don't make good pets."

Ace grunted. Riches weren't in his background, either. Surely Randee's down-to-earth personality meant superficial things were unimportant to her. Not that she'd be interested in a nerd like him, or that he'd ever act on anything.

"I recognized most of the people from PrimeRight, but not all of them."

Grateful for the change in topics, Ace asked, "You mean the multitude of attractive women?"

She smiled. "They seem to be having a lovely time at the party."

"Fritz always has women flocking around him. They're drawn like moths to a financially abundant flame."

"Money has that effect on some people."

"Fritz would be the exception to that assumption. He buys only the best of everything, but he's also the most pragmatic and loyal guy I've ever known." Why was he defending Fritz's honor? "I'm afraid my party personality is done for the night, so I came to retrieve my constant companion." He patted the briefcase on his lap.

"Okay, I'm ready to leave whenever you are," Randee replied.

Ace shook his head. "Please don't feel like you need to go just because I'm a killjoy. Fritz will have the limo take you home."

"Are you kidding? I'm ready to be makeup-free in my sweatpants." Randee slid onto the adjacent chair and kicked off a silver sandal, wiggling her painted toes.

An unfamiliar sense of relief that she wouldn't be staying at the party with Fritz surged through him. What was wrong with him? "These events wear me out. The introvert in me is screaming right now."

Randee laughed. "Not into small talk and socializing?"

"No, especially when Fritz parades me like a prize cow in front of strange people."

She gave him an understanding nod. "I'm sure he means well. Will he be upset that we're leaving so soon?"

Ace cringed. He'd never hear the end of it from Fritz if he scooted out early. And he'd really be in trouble if he left prior to the big surprise. "Good point."

"It's a nice night. How about taking a walk on the patio to delay our departure?" she suggested.

The notion sprang to mind, and before he reasoned it away, Ace blurted, "I have a better idea. Do you like horses?"

Randee tilted her head, and soft light captured the brilliant blue of her widened eyes. "That was random. But sure?"

He jumped up, excitement building. "Super. The only caveat is Fritz cannot catch us, or we'll be forced back to the party."

"Roger that." She stepped into her sandals and bit her lip, drawing his attention there.

Randee was attractive, intelligent and way out of his league. Ace swallowed, spun on his uncomfortable dress shoes and slowly opened the office door. He peered out, confirmed it was safe and led her to the veranda.

Once they reached the outdoors, he blew out a breath, eliciting a snicker from Randee. "You act like we just completed a covert operation."

"Believe me, getting away from Fritz without being seen qualifies." He sat on the stone patio wall and threw his legs over the side, then gently helped her over.

Descending the steep hill, they strolled through the valley of lush carpeted grass that spanned acres of land. A full moon hung heavy in the sky like a giant night-light. Fritz's home butted against the rolling hills bordering the east and a grove of trees to the north. The urge to hold Randee's hand was strong. Ace clutched the briefcase, grateful for the distraction to occupy him.

"This property is unbelievably gorgeous," Randee said.

Doesn't compare to you. Ace paused. The words had boomeranged in his brain and for a moment, he worried he'd spoken them aloud. Gauging Randee's lack of reaction, he hadn't. She appeared intrigued by the walk, oblivious to his disconcertion.

"Are you coming?" she prodded.

Ace gulped. "Yes, ma'am."

At the bottom of the valley, a trail of tiny lights led to the rocky path paving the way to an elaborate horse stable with mahogany-colored wood, accented by dark brown borders and a peaked roof. A covered entrance on the side resembled a fancy carport, and a soft luminescence emanated from the loft's three decorative windows.

As they neared the stables, he asked, "Do you know how to ride?"

"No."

"Me, either." He pushed wide the white-painted door, and they were greeted by the sweet scent of earth and hay mingling with something unpleasant.

Their footsteps echoed on the oak planks. A glow from the elaborate iron sconces provided ambient light over the immaculate stable. Long rows of stalls along one side were secured by black gates, and a set of leather saddles sat prepared on a block of straw at the far end.

A horse whinnied, and Randee moved toward the center stall. "Hello there. Oh, she has the gentlest brown eyes and longest lashes I've ever seen," she said.

"This is Mercy," Ace said, joining her.

Randee slid her fingers along the horse's muzzle. "You know her name, but you don't know how to ride?"

"I enjoy coming out here to talk—er, hang with them." He blinked and avoided her gaze, feeling more awkward teenager than grown man.

Thankfully, Randee changed topics. "How many are there?"

"Just two. Mercy." The click of hooves sounded against the wood, then another horse appeared from the next stall. "And this is Justice. He's a little nosy."

"Interesting names—" Randee lifted her hand, silencing

him as if she was listening to some invisible voice. Her casual position morphed, and she visibly stiffened. "What?" She averted her gaze, pressing a finger against her ear.

"Who are you talking to?" She shook her head and rushed past him to the stable window, wafting her sweet fragrance and temporarily interrupting his concentration.

He took gradual steps toward her and leaned closer, peering outside. "What's wrong?"

She tugged him down, her lips in a thin line, jaw set. And a Glock in hand.

He did a double take. "And where did you get that?"

She gripped his arm. "Ace, we need to go."

"Where? Why? What's gotten into you?" Randee's lack of response motivated Ace to find out for himself. He slid up enough to see out of the window again, this time catching the quick movement of shifting shadows along the tree line near the house. His focus transferred to the glimmer bouncing off the intruders' weapons, AK-47s and MP5s. Serious firepower. Dread and fear swarmed him like terrorizing locusts. When would the nightmare end with this project? Where was the ATF? Why weren't they protecting him? "They're back."

"Yes."

"If those folks in the house are in danger—" Ace swallowed hard "—we can't just leave them. We need to call the police. We have to help, not run away like cowards."

"The people at the party aren't the ones in danger. You and I are, and we don't have the weapons necessary to hold them off."

He studied her. "And you're aware of this how?"

An expression he couldn't quite explain, something between irritation and fear, passed over her face.

Randee ignored his question and pushed him aside, locking the door. "Do you know the grounds?" She blocked the exit with her body, again tilting her head. Her eyes widened. "Got it."

Whatever or whoever she heard in her mind elevated Ace's nervousness. He placed his hands on her shoulders. "Got what? Who are you talking to? Are you holding me hostage?"

"I'm saving your life. Is there another way out of here?" Randee stepped away from his touch.

"No." He turned and spoke to her back as she inspected the stable. "What are you looking for?"

"Never mind, there's no time. We need to hide."

Agitation at her dismissiveness erupted Ace's impatience. "Let them have the briefcase! I'm sick of this! They're not going to stop until they take Ghost or kill me or both. I won't hide, and I'm not running away. I'm done." He gripped the door handle.

Randee rushed to his side and placed her hand over his, shaking her head. "Ace. I understand what you're thinking and feeling. But we have to hide. If those men get a hold of Ghost...please, we can't let that happen." Her voice pleaded, but the gun she held said she wouldn't take no for an answer.

He wasn't stupid. He was fully aware of the ramifications of the criminals obtaining Ghost. With resignation, he released the knob and glanced up at the thin wooden ladder at the far side that led to the hayloft. "There's no place to go but up." The comment reminded him of a childhood Sunday school lesson on prayer. *Lord, if ever we needed help, it's now.*

"We have a major problem and too many intruders. Get Ace and Ghost out of here," Sergio's last command in Randee's earpiece gave her indisputable instructions. His words declared what she'd feared most. Something had delayed the ATF backup, which meant Malte had discovered the takedown mission. A leak in the bureau? Worse, her earpiece had gone silent, eliminating any communication with her team. Had they been compromised? She pressed her hand against her ear. "Advise status?" she said in one final desperate attempt.

Ace shot her a quizzical frown.

No response from Sergio or Wesley. No sounds at all. Could they still hear her? Were she and Ace safe in the stables or more vulnerable? She was on her own to get Ace to safety. There were no other options.

"We have to hide out somewhere until—" She hesitated, clinging to the thin thread of hope that backup would arrive in time.

Men's voices carried closer to the stables, vague but increasing in decibel. Malte's cronies were coming. She'd counted six in total, positioned around the home and blocking access to the vehicles. She glanced again at the horses. "Too bad neither of us can ride," she said more to herself than Ace.

"I could internet search how to saddle a horse, but I don't think we actually have time for that."

A grin tugged at Randee's lips despite the seriousness of the moment.

They needed to prepare to fight.

The comfort of her training kicked in. "Look for anything that might serve as a weapon and stay down."

Randee dropped to a squat and moved closer to the window. Two men dressed in plaid closed the distance, running across the grassy lawn and carrying MP5s.

Ace returned to her side holding a pitchfork. "Will this work?"

She grimaced. "Keep it close, but it's not much against their weapons."

"How many are there?"

"Two headed this way," she said on the off chance her mic was working. She checked her Glock. Still fully loaded.

She had one gun and no extra magazines. An insufficient match for the arsenal Malte's men had brought. And no doubt, if anyone heard gunfire, more of the intruders would descend on them. Worse, the attention might bring the oblivious partygoers outside, placing them in danger. No, she'd draw in the approaching invaders and take them by surprise. "I need a better vantage point."

Ace seemed to consider her question, taking far too long to respond.

She startled as he gripped her arm and tugged her toward the ladder at the rear. "We need to climb up to the hayloft."

She locked her feet in place. Surely he was joking. "No, they'll have us trapped."

One of the horses whinnied in reply.

"Check out the stable," a man's voice carried from outside.

Ace pulled harder on her arm. "Now, Randee. We don't have any other choices."

She lifted the edge of her evening gown and ascended the rickety ladder built for looks and not for usage. Grateful to disembark at the top, she moved to the side and swatted the long streams of spiderwebs caressing her bare skin.

"I'm passing you the briefcase," Ace said.

Randee hoisted the heavy item and set it beside her.

"Take this, too."

The pitchfork's lengthy wooden handle appeared, and she grasped hold of the tool, placing it next to the case. Ace climbed up to join her, his broad shoulders barely clearing the restrictive opening.

Randee took inventory of the expansive space, apparently used for housing old saddles and leftover gadgets. Her background didn't include farm life, and the rusted tools hanging in a macabre decorative style on the wall gave the loft a medieval atmosphere. She shivered involuntarily and wrapped her arms around her torso. The weight of her Glock gripped in her hand drew her back to the present.

Ace slipped beside her and paused. "If we're super quiet, they'll never know we're here."

"We can hope." If only she had a window to keep watch on the approaching intruders. Better yet, a place where they could escape the creepy loft. She spotted large hay bales stacked like blocks near a square cutout on the opposite wall. Randee pointed. "What's that?"

"Hay door."

Yes. They had a way out. She started toward it, her steps careful and soft across the slats.

Ace grasped her arm and shook his head. "Randee, it's just a big window for tossing out hay. There are no steps or ladder."

"See if there's a rope or something we can use to lower ourselves to the ground. It's our only exit."

The rattle of the door handle below froze them in place.

"It's locked," a man outside said. "Someone's in there."

"Where's the key?" a second asked, sounding more like a juvenile than an adult.

"We don't need a key."

"Go behind those bales," Randee ordered.

Ace grimaced, opened his mouth to argue, then clamped it shut again and crept around the massive blocks of hay. She crouched beside him and lifted her Glock, aiming at the top of the ladder.

A blast followed by the slamming of the door against the wall evoked another whinny from the horses.

Ominous footsteps echoed. "Come out, Mr. Steele. We only want the prototype."

If only the loft floor weren't so well built, she could've

seen through the slats. Consequently, it would've also provided a way for the men to see her, too.

Randee steadied her gun. She'd take them out as they ascended.

"Hey, what's this?"

A pause.

"An earring."

Randee's hand flew to her ear. She'd lost one of her earpieces. Great. And if those goons figured out it was the audio that connected her to Sergio...

"You can't run. There's no way out. Don't make us climb up there after you."

Silence.

"Ready or not..."

"Here we come," the other finished.

Randee's arm shook with adrenaline and anticipation. Cornered in the loft with no escape route meant her timing had to be perfect or they were dead. She blinked, allowing her eyes to adjust to the dim light.

The ladder creaked under the men's weight. The seconds ticked by in an agonizing delay until finally, a baseball cap peeked through the loft's opening.

Randee inhaled, stabilized her aim.

Ace's breathing beside her seemed to reverberate, announcing their hiding place.

As the man's plaid shoulders emerged, Randee fired.

He screamed and clutched his arm.

By his sudden disappearance, Randee assumed he'd forgotten to hold on to the ladder.

Several thuds followed by yelling confirmed the intruder's rapid plunge as he fell backward, apparently taking his friend right along to the bottom in a screaming, tumbling mess.

SEVEN

"This is all I could find." Ace tugged on a rope used to lower hay bales, ensuring it was secure, and pushed open the hay door. Whoever or whatever the pretty brunette was, her skills far exceeded self-defense. And who had she been talking to? He added her spectacular shooting to his ask-her-about-that-later list. "How do you feel about rappelling down the side?"

Randee's eyes widened—whether in doubt or surprise he wasn't sure. Her gaze rebounded from the loft opening, to the hay door, then back to him. "Go first, and I'll cover you."

A scurrying up the ladder said an intruder—most likely the one without a gunshot wound—was coming.

An argument lingered on his lips, but her stiffened stance and the hard set of her jaw conveyed her nonnegotiable order. Gripping the briefcase handle, he made a single-handed, incredibly awkward descent from the second floor. A new appreciation for his college rock-climbing adventures with Fritz bounced to the forefront of his mind.

Rapid gunfire resonated from inside the stable, quickening his descent. His palm burned from the coarse threads. He released his hold and glanced up as his shoes struck the hard ground.

In a blur of sequined material, Randee dived out the hay door. She latched onto the rope and swung wide, narrowly avoiding the bullets whizzing around her. If not for the life-threatening circumstances, her graceful moves would've been a beautiful sight.

Plastered against the stable wall, Ace marveled at her expert precision as she rappelled at breakneck speed from the loft.

The shooter appeared from the hay door above and fired twice more.

Ace shielded his head with the bulletproof briefcase. A ricocheting bullet pinged too close to his hand, and he jerked free, then recovered the case before it hit the ground.

Randee tugged him to the front of the building and returned fire. "We've got more company."

He peered around the wall and saw more plaid-clothed men rushing down the hill toward them. Movement in his peripheral vision caught his attention, and he turned to the small window in the stable door. The intruder Randee had shot held his arm, his face drawn in a murderous glare as he bolted in Ace's direction.

Heart thudding against his ribs, Ace waited until the man reached the door.

Ace gripped the knob and thrust it open, smacking the assailant and knocking him to the floor.

"Get them!" the shooter screeched from his hayloft perch, obviously unable to see his partner splayed out inside the stable.

Ace searched the winding road, and his gaze traveled to the plethora of available vehicles in front of the mansion. His contemplation halted at the impossible logistics of getting into a car unseen and the number of intruders surrounding them. Were there more lying in wait?

"Is there another route out of here?" Randee released a second round of bullets.

"Possibly, but I need to look on the other side of the stable."

"Go, I'll hold them off."

Ace rushed along the wood walls until he reached the end of the building and peered around the corner. The old pickup sat parked beside the gardening shed a football field away. The bordering tree line sheltered the vehicle. They'd have to make a run for it, risking exposure, but the truck was their only form of transportation. The X factor was whether the engine started.

If nothing else, the change of location would provide a brief reprieve and temporary cover while they called the police. Ace patted the pocket where he kept his cell phone. He glanced down.

Gone.

He spun to face the stable. Had he lost his phone inside? When he'd rappelled? Or up at the house? Ace rushed to Randee's side. "We'll have to make a run for the pickup."

She nodded. "We have a small window before they realize what we've done. When I say go, lead the way and don't look back."

"Got it."

An explosion above drew his attention.

Partygoers streamed from Fritz's home, flooding the hillside in their fancy clothes like confetti at a parade. Fireworks lit up the night, providing a happy diversion.

Ace grinned. So that was Fritz's surprise. *Perfect timing, buddy.*

The sky blossomed into brilliant colors of red, blue and green, momentarily distracting the pursuing gunmen.

Randee peered around the stable wall again, then whispered, "Go!"

They sprinted to the truck. Each second of vulnerability added to the feeling of a super-slow-motion getaway as they dodged the low tree branches. Ace led the way through the forest surrounding the north portion of the property. The wooded region lay beyond the glow emanating from the mansion windows.

At last, they reached the pickup, and Ace tugged open the driver's door. Randee dived in and scooted to the passenger side. He passed her the briefcase, then slid his hand under the seat, searching for the key the gardener kept there.

He snagged the cold brass just as the shooters rounded the stable.

The fireworks continued above them, mimicking gunfire.

Ace joined Randee and slammed the door shut. "Pray it starts."

"Already did." She yanked him closer in an awkward lean across the bench seat.

Ace shielded his face with his left arm as glass rained from the shattered driver's-side window.

Randee stretched over him and returned fire. "Ready?"

He thrust the key into the ignition after several clumsy attempts, and the truck wheezed and sputtered, refusing to start.

"Hurry," she urged.

"I'm trying, but I need to reach the pedal, and I can't do that sitting like this."

She shot again. "Okay, I'll move, but you have to stay down."

"Got it."

They shifted positions, and Ace slouched in the driver's seat, barely able to see over the dash. In a simultaneous effort, he turned the key and pumped the gas. Movement in his peripheral vision had him glancing over. Several bullets struck the door and dashboard. With mad fury, he stomped on the pedal and tried starting the ignition again. "Come on, come on!"

Finally, the engine roared to life.

The men rushed toward them, inches from the pickup. Ace shifted into Drive, revving and bouncing along the uneven lawn. The jalopy's aged cushions absorbed none of the impact. He turned onto a minimum-maintenance dirt lane and aimed for the county road.

"How far to the highway?" Randee asked, twisting around to monitor the pursuers.

"About four miles, but I'm going a different way in case those creeps are waiting for us."

"Good idea." She sat upright and snapped on her seat belt.

"Call the police."

"Hand me your phone. I left my clutch in the office."

Ace groaned and thrust his head back, inadvertently smacking it against the hard plastic. "I lost mine somewhere between the veranda and here."

"Great. Did you know about the fireworks?"

"No. Fritz told me he had a surprise, but I never even considered that option. Leave it to him to have perfect timing. Where should I go? Straight to the cops?"

"No!" Her response was too emphatic. "We need as much distance as possible from those men. Just drive opposite of wherever we are."

Ace worked his hands over the steering wheel. The truck rumbled, picking up speed as they descended into the valley of the rolling hills, then grumbling in protest as they ascended the next rise.

The adrenaline rush that had propelled him only moments before was fading fast. They rode in silence for several miles until Ace reached the paved county road.

Cold October air filtered in through the vents, and Randee wrapped her arms around her torso. Ace switched the temperature control to the heater mode and in a graceless bungling attempt, wiggled out of his tuxedo coat—one he'd rented but would be forced to buy after this. He pulled his arm free and passed it to her. "Sorry, a gentleman would've thought of that a long time ago."

Her fingers grazed his as she took the proffered jacket. "Thank you. The running kept me warm, but the temperature dropped ten degrees out of nowhere."

She gave him an appreciative smile, which he returned before concentrating on the road again.

"Any ideas where we could go? Somewhere away from Omaha. We need to change clothes and get more ammunition and guns. If Malte continues pursuing us, my Glock won't be enough to hold them off."

Ace considered the request. His apartment wasn't an option, but if they would be gone, he needed to take care of Rocko. He'd call his next-door neighbor, Mrs. O'Malley, and ask her to check on his cat. Except he had no phone.

The only place that came to him was the last place on the planet he'd want to go.

He sighed. "My parents' ranch in Hollow Hills."

Randee's face softened. "You wouldn't mind?"

Why would she think he'd mind? She couldn't possibly know about Cara's murder. He'd shared nothing, yet his gut told him Randee knew a lot more than she let on. "My folks are snowbirds and travel to Arizona in early October. They desert the ranch until they return in April."

"Works for me, but we can't stay there long. We have to keep moving." Randee wrapped herself in a hug.

Easy for her to say. She had no clue how stepping into

his family's home brought back the overwhelming guilt and self-condemnation. Anger, sorrow and irritation swirled in his stomach, a combined wave of emotions. Within seconds he chose the most familiar, anger.

Before he weighed his words, he blurted, "I like to think I'm open-minded and reasonable, but I'm over this whole experience. It's obvious you're helping me, and I appreciate you saving my life. But whoever you are, Randee Jones—if that's your real name—I'm not thrilled about being lied to. I deserve the truth."

"I agree." Randee didn't face him or refute his words. She also didn't elaborate.

Impatience ruled his tongue. "Who are these men trying to kill me and take Ghost?"

She sighed and swiveled in her seat. "Titus Malte's followers. He's an eccentric and wealthy local militia leader."

Images of crazed commando groups crawling out from underground camouflaged bunkers on acres of land came to his mind. "You lost me. How would a man like that have any information about Ghost?"

"Ace, you deserve answers, and I want to give them to you. But for now, can we leave it at Malte wants Ghost and will do whatever it takes to obtain it?"

"Absolutely not. You must think I'm stupid or gullible."

"That isn't true."

"I'm not pretending to be okay with any of this."

"I'm not asking you to, just give me time until…" She turned away.

"Until what?" He pulled over to the side of the road.

Randee spun to face him, her hand on the dashboard. "Ace, we need a lot more miles between us and Malte's men. Continue yelling at me, as long as you also keep driving."

"We're not moving until you tell me the truth." His chest

tightened with each word. He knew she was right, but her refusal to share information required drastic measures.

"I promise to talk, if you drive."

Ace considered a standoff with her but the dread of the men catching up with them forced him back onto the road.

Randee released a long sigh. "If Malte steals Ghost and the plans, he'll have the capability to outfit his followers with custom weapons. They'd have an army equipped to infiltrate government buildings or public places and do irreparable damage. This goes far beyond you and me."

"Obviously."

Her eyes flashed and her lips thinned into a narrow line. "I realize you're on the outer loop, but understand that all that's happened has been for your safety. When I'm able to answer more of your questions, I will. For now, be satisfied in knowing there's a team of people determined to keep you alive, and it's my highest priority."

Randee studied Ace. His jaw was set in a hard line, and his eyes never detoured from the windshield. Everything within her wanted to reassure him that she wasn't being contrary. By keeping her professional distance, she was protecting him.

Yet her conscience agreed with him. He deserved the truth after all they'd endured, and she wanted nothing more than to give him answers. A premature revelation of the lingering fragments of her anonymity would leave her completely vulnerable. Though doubtful Ace was collaborating with Malte, he wasn't out of the realm of suspicion. What if he was pretending ignorance about the men at the house? There was a strong possibility Ace and Malte were in on the raid. Until she found evidence stating otherwise, she wouldn't overshare.

She needed more information, and that might require

an exchange of confidences to secure his trust. Until she extended that olive branch, he'd never tell her anything.

Her mind played a tug-of-war between doubting Ace and her confidence that he wasn't the spy. He'd been in the home office removing the briefcase from the safe. If she hadn't surprised him, he would've had the opportunity to escape with Ghost.

No. Surely he wasn't involved in the raid. Even if he was an award-worthy actor, he wouldn't play innocent while Malte's men attempted to kill them. Would he?

She quashed the debate. Ace wouldn't have acted with such insidious malice. He wasn't Malte's spy.

So, what instinctively kept her from confessing everything to him?

Randee exhaled in relief at the bright green gas station sign. Antiquated in appearance, it was questionable it had cell phones. However, it was open for business, and she prayed they had a landline. "Drive in there. I'll go inside to make the call."

Ace didn't respond. He pulled into the parking area, and she hopped out before he asked any more questions.

The woman behind the counter seemed to study her, and Randee was suddenly aware of her appearance. She worked to keep her tone light. "Hi, there. I'm sorry to bother you, but may I please use your phone?"

A concerned frown on the woman's weathered face was followed by suspicion in her furrowed brow. "You all right, girl?"

Randee tucked a stray tendril behind her ear. "Oh, yes. Just need to make a call."

The attendant gave her a wary once-over before gesturing for her to come around the counter. She pointed to the phone but didn't move aside. "Make it quick."

Randee moved into the cramped space and by the woman's

determination to stay near her, it was obvious privacy wasn't an option. She blocked the keypad to prevent the cashier from seeing and eagerly punched in Ishi's number.

Three rings, then it went to voice mail. Why wasn't she answering? "Ishi, it's Randee." She glanced up at the nosy attendant's probing gaze and considered her words, choosing them with caution. "Lost the guys and my phone at the party. Hope you've heard from them and have some good news for me. We had some…vehicle issues—"

The cashier cleared her throat and motioned for Randee to hurry up. She turned her back, but that wouldn't deter her eavesdropping.

"Um, so Ace and I are going on up north to the ranch." Randee prayed Ishi understood her cryptic message and would send help. "I'm hoping you'll meet us there or at least send the guys that way. I'll call as soon as we arrive." She disconnected and stepped back. "Thank you."

Occupied with stacking items in the display, the cashier didn't regard Randee. "Mmm-hmm."

Exiting the store, Randee's steps were weighted with disappointment as she trudged to the truck where Ace sat, erect with hope etched in his face. "Are the police coming?"

She slammed the door shut. "No, and we need to keep going."

"What? Why?"

The attendant watched from the window. "Ace, we're drawing attention to ourselves. Please just keep driving."

He grunted and pulled away from the gas station. "That's crazy. Why wouldn't we notify the cops?"

"Trust me on this."

"My father always said never trust anyone who says, 'trust me.'"

"Ace." Randee rubbed her forehead. What did they do now?

"Who'd you call then?"

"Ishi, but I couldn't get a hold of her. The attendant wouldn't leave my side, so I had to leave a message. I'll have to try again."

"Who's Ishi?"

"The only person who can help us at the moment."

"Randee—"

She swallowed the lump in her throat. What were her next steps? They hadn't exactly planned for this haphazard a night. Her chest squeezed with worry. Were Sergio and Wesley okay? *Please Lord, let them be safe.*

There was no way Ace believed she was an ordinary accountant with great fighting skills. But if Malte's men got away and her team had been compromised, or worse, where did that leave her? Too many unknowns and questions that offered no answers.

Randee groaned. How had the plan gone wrong? Why hadn't she stayed and fought? She'd abandoned Wesley and Sergio by obeying her commander's instructions. Tears threatened, and she shoved them down. No. She'd hold on to any thread of hope until she knew for sure. Then there would be plenty of time to grieve.

"Randee?"

Her name on Ace's lips embraced her, dissolving her reserve, and against her better judgment, she glanced up. Her will to remain reticent disintegrated at the pleading depth in his blue eyes. The concern and worry that played in his expression drove another nail through her deceptive heart. She longed to look away but couldn't bring herself to deflect her gaze.

"Please talk to me. You want me to trust you, but you

won't do the same." His tone was gentle, though he spoke louder over the growling engine.

He was right, but confessing meant giving up hope that the mission was still intact. Sergio and Wesley might've arrested Malte's men. The case was active as far as she was concerned. "Just give me time to figure out what should happen next."

"Fine, but at least tell me the truth about the gun. And your combat skills."

Randee remained silent.

"Okay, why can't we go to the police?"

She shifted in her seat, uncomfortable physically and emotionally. "I will explain. Later."

"Who are you? Really?"

Ace's question sent a shiver down her back. She'd longed to answer that for years. Who was she? Goal-driven. Lonely. Afraid of real relationships. The thought of baring her battered soul to him terrified her. But that wasn't what Ace was asking, and she knew it.

Frost built up on her window. Something in the shifting winds predicted weather was coming. The unusual warmth could change in a heartbeat in Nebraska.

Hollow Hills gave them the necessary distance from Omaha and Malte. It was also too far for a hasty arrival of backup. Ironically, the remoteness provided solace or increased the reality of danger…and it was their only plan right now.

A flutter of sparse snowflakes peppered the windshield.

"That came out of nowhere," Ace commented, switching on the defrost.

"How much farther?" She snuggled down under the tuxedo coat.

"About an hour."

"Do you visit your parents' place often?" Randee was well aware of the Steeles' strained relationship.

"No. We've…grown apart."

"I'm not close to my mother, either. Not since my father passed away." Why was she offering personal information to him?

"I go out to their house to check on things while they're gone."

"Did you grow up there?" Her imposter inquisition felt silly, but PrimeRight accountant Randee Jones wouldn't know Ace's history. He'd already surmised she'd faked her identity, but maintaining her ruse prevented her from confessing too much about herself.

"Yes. My parents inherited the ranch from my grandparents. It's been in the family for several generations."

"Do they farm?" Why was she interrogating him? Because if she kept him talking, he wouldn't ask her questions.

"Not anymore. They rent the land out to a larger farming operation."

"And I'm guessing you didn't want to follow in the business?"

Ace flexed his jaw, and Randee debated whether she'd pushed too far. "No. I prefer science, which my parents despised. It added to their already low opinion of me." He turned on the radio, concluding any further discussion.

An acoustic rendition of a familiar song carried from the dashboard. A strange addition to the stressful atmosphere.

Wasn't Ace every parent's dream child? His background check had revealed a perfect college grade point average, squeaky-clean driving record and exceptional credit score. The man lived an impeccable life. Never as much as a speeding ticket or an overdue library book. But Randee's experience confirmed that commendations mattered little when it came to the fickleness of family.

She wanted to quiz him and learn more about what made Ace in his personal life. But her main curiosity was rooted in the details regarding his sister's murder. Based upon the way he had shut down, this wasn't the time.

The ride took forever and still ended too soon. Ace drove onto the long dirt road leading to the ranch-style brick home. Sensor lights came on as they approached.

She turned to him. His hands gripped the steering wheel as if he were holding on for dear life.

His willingness to take her to the Steeles' home touched and worried her. Was she getting too close to this quagmire of a man?

A twinge of guilt for hiding her knowledge regarding his past niggled at her. Randee opened her mouth to speak, then decided against it. No. Telling him meant revealing her true identity. Until she had verification of her team's status, she'd remain undercover. Yet why did she feel so guilty?

Ace pulled up to the house, beaming headlights on the attached garage. The snow's intensity increased, and the flakes fell faster in heavy, thick masses blanketing the ground in briskly accumulating layers of white powder. The wind whipped against the pickup, spraying the snow in a fierce mist that prevented Randee from seeing more than two feet ahead. She released her seat belt and placed her hand on the handle.

"Stay in the truck. I'll pull into the garage," Ace said, shifting into Park.

Reluctantly, she slid back.

He got out, moved to the building, and entered a code into the keypad; the door emitted a groan. The overhead light illuminated the snow blasting around the pristine garage.

She would clear the area, no doubt adding to Ace's suspicions of her. Too bad. It was mandatory.

He returned to the truck and pulled inside, then shut off the engine.

"It's doubtful anyone knows we're here, but just in case, let me go first," Randee said, placing her hand on his arm. She braced herself for his argument. She was running out of reasonable and believable explanations.

Instead, Ace nodded and hefted the briefcase from the floorboard.

Palming her Glock, Randee stepped from the truck and entered the house through the attached door. Ace fell behind her and flipped on the light in the mudroom. He hung back, allowing her to clear the kitchen and living area.

The faint hint of lavender lingered, and she spotted the plug-in air freshener in the outlet near the sofa. The recently updated interior had a simple open floor plan. Apparently, minimalist was the style for the Steele family. Large rectangular rugs covered the hardwood floors, adding splashes of reds and grays. No framed prints or decorative fixtures adorned the walls, no personal effects on the mantel. The home was as impersonal as a hotel. A black double-door gun cabinet stood in the far corner of the living room.

Randee moved to the farthest bedroom at the end of the hallway and opened the door, pausing in her tracks. She'd stepped back in time, specifically the nineties. A white canopy bed, matching nightstands and dresser along with a pink throw rug decorated the space. Pictures of a beautiful girl smiling and laughing adorned the walls.

Cara's room.

Randee continued, captured by a picture on the bulletin board. The young woman's arms slung over a nerdy-looking teen boy.

Had to be Ace. The shocking blue of his eyes beamed back at her from behind the thin-framed glasses. His wide, brace-filled grin screamed pride and joy.

Nothing had changed, and it appeared the family had enshrined their only daughter's bedroom. Not uncommon for grieving parents after losing a child. Though Cara's death had occurred over two decades prior.

She peered under the bed, checked the closet full of clothes and shoes, then turned and exited the room, closing the door behind her.

Randee continued into the other sparsely decorated bedrooms. Each held a queen-size bed, dresser and nightstand. No decorations and nothing extravagant in the home. Once more, she contrasted Ace's and Fritz's lifestyles.

Upon completion of clearing the property, she returned to where Ace stood facing the living room gas fireplace.

"If you wouldn't mind, a fire would be great."

He spun around, the ever-present briefcase at his feet. "Uh. Sure." He flipped the switch on the wall. Flames sprang to life.

Randee surveyed the space again. How interesting that the family left Cara's room so precisely intact while the rest of the house revealed nothing personal about the occupants. "You said your folks have guns here?" She pointed to the cabinet.

Ace nodded, then walked past her to the master bedroom. She contemplated following him but refrained. He returned a few seconds later carrying a duffel bag and a key. Unlocking the cabinet, he tugged open both doors, revealing several rifles, a handgun and an abundance of ammunition. Randee approached and helped load the weapons into the duffel.

When they'd finished, she said, "I think we should get moving. It's not safe for us to stay here."

"Are you hungry?" he asked, ignoring her comment, weariness in his tone. The lines on his face conveyed exhaustion.

She slipped onto the red leather couch and set her gun on the side table. Maybe he needed a moment to regroup. She'd give him that and then insist on their departure. "A little. Is there a landline?" She glanced around the home, hoping she'd missed it in her perusal.

Ace snorted. "My parents only use their cell phones. They don't even have internet access."

Disappointment washed over her. No chance of trying to reach Ishi from the Steele ranch. They had to leave and find a phone. Randee stood and walked to the windows, pulling back the blinds. The snow continued to fall at an increased speed with thick, heavy flakes. "It's really coming down out there."

Ace flipped on the television. "No cable or satellite, but we get a few local stations."

Switching the channels, he turned up the volume when the program returned from a commercial break. The meteorologist informed them that a cold current had covered the area and a large accumulation of snow was expected throughout the night along with extensive winds. Blizzard and whiteout conditions.

Ace moved into the kitchen and opened cupboards.

"Doesn't the pickup have four-wheel drive?"

"Nope, just a rear-wheel drive beater." He ducked behind the dark wood pantry door and mumbled, "Hmm. Slim pickings."

Worry tugged at Randee. "Maybe we should try to venture out to the store before the storm gets worse?"

"Blizzard conditions continue to gain momentum. The

Nebraska state patrol urges people to stay off the roads to-night," the weather forecaster piped in from the television.

"I don't think that's a good idea. With the wind picking up, it'll make for a whiteout. And nothing in Hollow Hills is open this time of night, anyway."

Randee slumped back into the seat cushions. "I'd like to get an early start then."

"Absolutely." He disappeared down the hall and re-turned a few minutes later. "Thought you'd need these," he replied, holding out a small stack of folded clothing.

She reached for the proffered items, locking gazes with him. His rich blue eyes, shadowed by long thick eyelashes, pulled her in.

Had he been this attractive all along? The man was downright gorgeous. Warmth radiated up her neck, and she hoped she hadn't spoken her assessment aloud.

Ace thrust the clothes at her and jolted her to the pres-ent situation. She caught the clothing in an awkward grasp, grazing his hands, and looked down at the light purple woman's hoodie and matching sweatpants.

"They'll be too big, but it'll be better than wearing that." He gestured toward her dress, turning Randee's attention to her bedraggled attire.

Embarrassment hung on her shoulders like the once-beautiful sequined fabric clinging unattractively in a disheveled and shredded mess around her ankles. She clutched the warm clothes against her chest. "Thank you."

His expression softened slightly, and he blurted, "Oh, you'll need socks, too." In an about-face, he headed to the master bedroom and returned seconds later with a pair of fuzzy white-and-purple microfiber socks wrapped with a red ribbon.

Randee smiled. He'd matched the colors to the hoodie. Ace was a thoughtful man. She took the soft footwear, and he stepped back, shoving his hands into his tuxedo pants pockets. "There's a pile in my mother's drawer if you want a different set. I buy her a pair every Christmas just so she can ignore them. But at least they're clean and not worn."

"These are great. Thanks again." She shifted from one foot to the other. "May I use your restroom?"

"Sure, down the hall…although you already know that, don't you?" The hardness had returned to his tone, and he moved to the kitchen.

Randee pushed off the couch and walked to the bathroom. She paused. Were they safe? She shook off the concern. Malte's men wouldn't dare attack out here. How would they even have an indication of her and Ace's location? Regardless, they wouldn't stay long. Just enough to wait out the storm. Then they'd warm up, change clothes and maybe grab something to eat.

They were out of danger.

For now.

EIGHT

Ace's frustration simmered like the soup he stood heating on the stove—low, steady…and working up to a boil. Why wouldn't Randee tell him anything? She'd fought the overabundance of attackers they'd faced the past couple of days. So, what was she hiding?

He stirred the soup, wafting an appetizing scent. Unlike the mysterious Randee, there was no mystery in the slightly expired preservative-filled contents. It also happened to be one of the few edible items left in the cupboards.

Food was the last thing on his mind. He'd only prepared the meal to thwart Randee's attempts at small talk. She'd taken the hint and opted to change clothes in the bathroom, leaving him alone to ponder his racing thoughts.

He turned to grab bowls from the cabinet and caught a shadow in his peripheral vision. Ace spun, connecting with a blow to the side of his head. He stumbled backward and reached for the counter. Regaining his footing, he faced and sized up his opponent.

The man stood over six feet tall and nearly as wide, filling the darkened entrance of the mudroom. The Ruger aimed in Ace's direction held his undivided attention.

"I been waitin' for you." The intruder's voice sounded as if he gargled rocks on a regular basis.

"Who are you?" Ace flattened against the counter and inched toward the boiling pan on the stove.

"Stop yer movin'!" He hefted the Ruger higher and took a step closer. "Where's the gun?"

Ace refrained from glancing at the briefcase and the duffel bag with his father's guns sitting beside the sofa, not visible from the man's point of view.

The sound of running water reminded him of Randee's presence. She'd be vulnerable if she walked into the hallway unsuspecting of their new visitor. Ace determined to keep the man talking, hoping she'd hear them and stay in the bathroom. He forced a calm to his voice and spoke louder. "I said, who are you?"

"You ain't askin' the questions. I am. Gimme the gun or I'll kill you and your girlfriend." The trespasser stepped forward, exposing more of his appearance to the light. His thick brown beard covered everything the hat didn't.

"Put your gun down very slowly," Randee said.

Shifting to keep an eye on the intruder, he glimpsed her wearing the hoodie and sweatpants. For all the issues he had with her over the course of the evening, he had to admit, her timing was impeccable, as was her rock-steady hold on her Glock.

The man snorted. "No, lady, you need to put your gun down, or I'm shootin' your boyfriend here."

"You know I won't allow that," Randee answered.

"That's downright cute. She your bodyguard?" His question dripped with sarcasm.

Ace clenched his fists, forcing his energy into his plan rather than replying to the snide comment.

"I'm warning you once more, drop your gun or I'll shoot," Randee said.

The intruder took her challenge and stepped closer. "Lady, you ain't got—"

Lunging, Ace grasped the pan's handle and swung.

The boiling soup scalded the intruder. He hollered and threw up his hands in a protective stance, dropping the Ruger.

Randee rushed forward to grab the gun, but the man gave a guttural growl and thrust his elbow into her face. She stumbled back and shielded her bleeding nose. Her gun toppled to the ground and skidded across the tile floor. Too close to the intruder.

Ace launched, landing a punch to the invader's ample middle and doubling him over with a hefty whoosh of exhaled breath.

"Now you done it!" He reached into his pocket and withdrew a second pistol, then ducked into the mudroom.

Randee grabbed her gun, and Ace tugged her around the corner into the living room. Bullets pelted the drywall as the intruder continued firing from his vantage point. The front door loomed opposite where they stood, and reaching it required running into the open. Ace pointed to the exit, but Randee shook her head and gestured for him to get down.

She flattened herself against the wall separating the living room and kitchen. The briefcase still sat next to the sofa. Without thinking about the consequences, Ace lunged for the case.

A bullet impaled the cushion inches from his leg.

He dived across the room, clutching the briefcase, and skidded beside Randee where she continued to return fire.

The air went still. Too still.

Had Randee killed the man? Curious, he moved behind her and peered around the corner. Was he gone, or hiding and waiting to attack?

"Stay here," Randee mouthed before cautiously approaching the kitchen.

Ace ignored her, clutched the briefcase and ran the opposite direction to the front entrance, hoping to trap the intruder between them. He yanked open the door and sucked in a breath. An icy gust of wind and blinding snow smothered him and eliminated any view he had of the outdoors.

The distant sound of an invisible engine roared to life and faded into the white abyss.

"He escaped out the garage window," Randee reported from behind him.

"He must've been driving something small. I'm guessing a UTV, which means he has cross-country access."

"We have to leave. Malte may send more of his men."

Ace closed the door. "Fine, but we need supplies in case we get stuck out there. And we're starting with better fitting clothes for you."

Randee glanced down and tugged at the sagging jogging pants. She'd rolled the waistband to keep them from falling off.

"Come on." He set down the briefcase and gestured for her to follow.

Randee fell into step without comment.

He paused with his hand on Cara's door, then entered and headed for the closet. With a sigh, he withdrew several pairs of pants and a blue-and-orange Broncos hoodie. "My sister was much closer to your build, and my mother doesn't keep many winter clothes since they're never here. Will any of these work?" He gestured toward the options laid out on the bed.

Randee hesitated, then lifted the first pair of jeans. "Ace, I don't want to intrude—"

"My parents have preserved my sister Cara's memory long enough. She's gone, and turning her bedroom into a shrine isn't going to bring her back. It makes little sense for you to wear clothes that are too big when these are available."

"But your folks—"

"—will be none the wiser. We'll wash and return them before they get home. Besides, I'll have to repair the bullet holes, anyway."

She grimaced. "Sorry about the damage."

"Yeah, those might be difficult to explain." He gave her a weak smile and turned, grabbing a pair of pink sneakers, then withdrew socks from Cara's dresser. "I'm sure her shoes will fit you, too." He stepped to the side. "I'll gather the rest of the supplies while you dress." He walked out of the room without giving her a chance to respond.

Ace walked to what used to be his room. They had removed everything except three pieces of furniture from his once-private domain. His mother had painted a fresh coat of boring and nondescript white over the place where his high school trophies, awards, posters and pictures had hung, now replaced by a void opposite him.

The renovations left his room bland and devoid of anything that might remind his parents he'd once existed here. The silent emphasis that he wasn't needed or wanted in their lives except from April to October when he checked on their house.

He dragged his old snow boots and winter coat from the closet. Surprised his mother hadn't donated them to Goodwill with all of his other things. He found jeans and a hoodie, then completed his cold-weather attire with a pair of gloves from the mudroom cabinets.

Randee met him in the kitchen as he filled a few bottles with water. He added them to the backpack he'd found along with matches, a first aid kit and a few blankets.

His focus landed on the developing bruise where the intruder's elbow had connected with her nose and eye.

Angry at the attacker and concerned for Randee, he said, "We'd better get something on that shiner."

Ace pulled open a drawer where his mother kept resealable bags. He withdrew the tray from the freezer and assembled an ice pack. Then he wet a towel and, dropping onto the seat next to her, he gently applied the compress to her face.

She winced, and he paused at the sudden nervousness fluttering throughout his chest. "Sorry." *That's the best you can think of to say?*

"It's okay, just a little tender and cold." Her smile was warm as she reached up, placing her hand on his to hold the ice. "Thank you."

Ace withdrew, instantly missing the contact with her. He snatched up the towel and dabbed at the drying blood around her nose. "At least it stopped bleeding," he said, unable to avert his gaze.

Even with the ugly darkness marring her beautiful face, she remained attractive. Her eyes were dark blue, like the sapphires his mother was once so fond of. He swallowed hard, forcing down the ill-timed memory that set him on edge. Without warning, his mouth went dry, and he struggled to swallow. He dropped the towel and jerked back. "Let me mop up this mess and we'll get out of here."

Randee quirked a brow, letting him know his abrupt change hadn't gone unnoticed.

He finished cleaning up the spilled soup, then walked into the living room and surveyed the damage. His gaze landed on the newest home renovation addition…the fireplace. The same place he'd found Cara's lifeless body slumped against the wall. The bland gray stone reminded him of his mother's cold words. "No one deserves to be happy, Ace. Least of all you. It's your fault she's gone, and I will never forgive you."

The suffocating atmosphere that always accompanied family memories rose again, and he longed to escape the home.

He hated this room.

Hated being here.

Hated knowing there was no sanctuary to go to.

"Ace?" The gentleness of Randee's voice jolted him back to the present.

Guilt shrouded him, twisting his stomach at the sight of her holding the ice pack against her eye. Once more he'd failed to protect a person he cared about.

The thought halted him.

How could he care about someone who'd failed to be honest with him? He knew nothing about Randee. He squelched the internal conversation with an irritated exasperation as he recalled her reluctance to tell him the truth. He was fighting an invisible foe with terrifying real attackers.

"What else can you tell me about this guy Malte?"

She looked down. "Right now, nothing."

Ace sighed, annoyed.

"Please know I'm doing my job."

"And what would that be? I'm tired of this game, and I'm not accepting your deflections for answers anymore. I want the truth."

She exhaled and paused, as if considering whether to say more. "Okay. I'm an ATF agent, working undercover to guard Ghost."

He blinked. That explained her skills, but not why she'd lied to him. He'd signed the government forms ad nauseam and none mentioned 24-7 protection. That would've been a benefit, not a deterrent. Unless...fresh irritation fueled his words. "There was nothing about the repeated attempts on my life in the contracts. If the ATF is so concerned about my welfare, why not tell me I have a bodyguard?"

Her hesitant response confirmed what he'd guessed.

"You're not guarding Ghost. You're watching me." He stormed past her and grabbed the briefcase from the floor. "You're worried I'll run off with my prototype or sell it to Malte."

Randee shook her head. "For the record, it's not *your* prototype. Ghost belongs to the ATF. Everyone's safety is at risk, as you've witnessed."

Embarrassment hardened his stomach, and the ground seemed to shift beneath his feet. The reality was, for the slightest moment, he'd stupidly considered Randee more than a coworker. She hadn't befriended him. She'd been assigned to watch him and report on his every move. The ATF hadn't placed its trust and confidence in his development of Ghost. It'd played him. She'd played him. Made him believe he was more important to the project than he really was. The ATF determined he was an incompetent drone incapable of handling a top secret assignment, so they'd sent him a babysitter.

Was Fritz in on it, too? Every insecurity and self-condemning voice bounced to the forefront of his mind, melding with the intruder's words. *That's downright cute. She your bodyguard?*

Desperate to escape the suffocating atmosphere, he blurted, "We need to leave. Now."

Randee averted her eyes, focusing on the TV screen where a thick red line across the bottom announced school and business closures. The small box on the right side indicated the counties and their varying degrees of winter weather advisories and warnings. She tamped down the anxiousness about traveling in the blizzard and snatched the duffel packed with the guns.

Ace turned off the TV, locked the front door and headed toward the garage.

"Guess it's only going to get worse before it gets better," she said, following him.

"Yeah," he grumbled.

They loaded the supplies into the truck, minimizing the already tight space.

She climbed in, and Ace slid behind the wheel. He turned the ignition, but nothing happened.

Grumbling, Ace got out and popped the hood. "You might as well go back inside where it's warm."

"Is something wrong?" Perhaps a dumb question considering the obvious, but talking to him went beyond walking on eggshells.

"Our visitor apparently messed with our ride."

Frustration oozed through Randee. Time was of the essence, and they were delayed again. Unfortunately, she knew nothing about vehicle repair. "How bad is it?"

He grunted from behind the hood. "Not permanently disabling. He cut a wire and tried to remove the distributor cap." She heard a few grumbles and other assorted noises.

Randee walked to his side. "Can I help?"

He glared. "No. Just give me a few."

She stepped out of his way and watched as he stalked to the back side of the garage, tugging open drawers until he found the tools he needed before returning to the vehicle.

Twenty minutes later, impatience building, Randee asked, "Sure you don't need anything?"

"I've got it," he grumbled.

She started to protest, then thought better of it. Arguing with him would only add to their already strained communications.

How had the intruder escaped in the blizzard? Randee surveyed the landscape. The ground was swept smooth by the winds, covering any tracks he might've left.

But there would be more of Malte's cronies to battle, she was sure of it. She glanced over her shoulder where Ace appeared to be finishing up, though she didn't dare ask.

What time was it, anyway? Excusing herself to the bathroom, Randee spotted the stove's clock. If they didn't get out of here soon, they'd be easy targets for Malte's next attempt. Ace had been working on the pickup for what seemed like forever, but it wasn't as if they had any other drivable options.

At last Ace started the engine, and Randee climbed in. He backed out of the garage, then jumped out to close the door using the external keypad. Snow pelted the truck, and Randee turned up the defrost. Had she been wrong to tell Ace the truth? No. He was angry, but he had the right to be. Still, the progress they'd made in getting to know each other was now buried behind a wall again.

He climbed in and slammed the door. They exited the driveway in a slow progression. The tires crunched on the snow, and the headlights illuminated the white flakes, making an almost-blinding approach to the road. Randee glanced in the side mirror as the Steele ranch faded in the distance.

She patted the hoodie pocket holding her Glock, unable to shake the guilt of wearing Cara's things, but everything fit perfectly. And as Ace had said, she'd launder and return them as soon as possible.

"Thank you," she mouthed, glancing at Cara's darkened bedroom window. Though they'd never met, a tenderness for the family torn apart by the girl's tragic death weighed heavily on her shoulders.

The Steeles had sterilized the home by removing everything personal, while Cara's room had been preserved as if she still lived there. All the irritation that she'd felt earlier evaporated. Randee closed her eyes and said a prayer for the parents aching from the loss of their daughter. Maybe in time, God would heal and restore their small family again.

Ace accelerated on the highway, causing the truck to fishtail on the icy road. To his credit, he recovered, and they continued their departure into the blowing snow. "For the record, I disagree with leaving in this weather, but I guess Malte knows our location so there are no other options. Where to now?"

Randee considered his question. "We need to get a phone. Where's the closest store?"

"Depends on which direction we go. Possibly in Randolph, although it's pretty late."

"Let's try that and if not, just keep going until we find an open one."

"Randolph is off the main highway."

"I'd prefer we take smaller county roads, so it's not as easy for Malte to follow us."

Ace snorted. "And more dangerous for us to travel."

"If you have a better suggestion, I'm open." She watched his expression, but he never took his eyes from the windshield.

"You're the expert, *Agent*." He spoke her title as though it was a bitter taste in his mouth, pricking her heart. "I'm having a hard time with this strange arrangement. I can't pretend you're Randee Jones, super accountant for Prime-Right. So would you at least tell me who you are?"

She sat up straighter and squared her shoulders. What could it hurt now? "Fair enough. My name is Miranda Jareau. Randee was my dad's nickname for me."

Ace's grip appeared to relax slightly on the steering

wheel. He held out one hand in an awkward offering. "Nice to meet you, Miranda Jareau."

With a small grin, she received his palm and gave him a strong shake. "Which do you prefer, Randee or Miranda?"

She shrugged. "Mother said Dad nicknamed me Randee as a consolation for having a daughter instead of a son."

Ace frowned. "Sounds like something my mom would say."

A strange bond hovered between them, a silent confirmation that Ace understood the pain of familial struggles.

"When we were deciding my PrimeRight alias, Randee came to mind, so I sort of reverted to it." She shifted, focusing on the flakes pelting the windshield in a mesmerizing pattern.

"Miranda's pretty, but Randee suits you."

The comment got her attention, and she glanced up with a sad smile, unable to think of anything to say. Randee longed for a reprieve from Malte's men and the comfort of her team's presence.

How long could she protect Ace and Ghost without their support?

NINE

A fresh concoction of complicated emotions—bitterness, anger, curiosity and embarrassment—rose in Ace's chest. Who was Miranda Jareau?

His curiosity overrode his anger, which meant he'd have to be nicer, and that came dangerously close to vulnerable. He also yearned to get to know her, except for his indignation at her continued deception.

However, they were stuck together, at least until they trudged their way back to…he wasn't even sure where they'd go. But one thing he knew, as soon as possible, he'd rid himself of the beautiful petite brunette with mad fighting skills.

Ace sighed. Randee was protecting him. Scratch that, it was her job to protect Ghost, the pet project and very bane of his existence.

What had Fritz thought when the fireworks ended? Had he noticed Randee and Ace were missing? Should he call? Would that endanger Fritz, or send Malte's men descending on him and Randee again? Fritz was the only family Ace had anymore. For all his pomp and circumstance, Fritz was nothing more than a scared child trying to prove his worth to an invisible and condemning force. His parents were so much like Ace's, demanding perfection, never satisfied with even the best achievements. And like Ace, Fritz struggled to please them and earn their favor along with everyone else's.

Ace had given up that fight. Mostly. Nothing he did would earn his parents' love. They'd stored their parental feelings when Cara died, taking their hurt and grief and stacking it into a combined disdain for their worthless son. After all, he'd failed to protect her. Regret for leaving that fateful night returned and with it the self-condemnation for selfishly sneaking out after his parents left for a party. All so he and Fritz could go to the movies too far away in the neighboring town's theater while he was supposed to be home with Cara. Typical of her loving big-sister ways, she'd promised to cover for him, unsuspecting her ex-boyfriend would visit.

Phillip had been arrested and convicted of stalking Cara. Upon the day of his parole release, he'd exacted his revenge. If he couldn't be with Cara, no one would.

Ace inhaled, desperate to ignore the memories while wanting to feel the pain afresh. The hurt reminded him of the importance of completing Ghost. Why had he agreed to this wretched project in the first place? The ATF ensured him Ghost was a step in preventing criminals from making illegal, untraceable 3-D printer guns. Whatever it took to achieve that goal and protect innocents like Cara, Ace promised to do. *Give me the strength to finish this, Lord. And protect me and Randee until we can pass this to the authorities.*

The notion that someone was watching him had Ace glancing over at Randee. Her hair framed her oval face in wavy cascades, giving her an almost impish appeal. Her wide eyes held a gentleness, and the urge to reach for her overwhelmed him. It didn't matter that she'd lied, or that she wasn't who she'd pretended to be. For the first time in his life, Ace understood why men did stupid things to win over a woman. Reasoning away the realities, in this place where his vulnerability exceeded common sense, he longed for someone's acceptance.

Randee smiled at him. "Thank you for braving the elements. I know there's not much I can do at the moment, but when this is over if there's anything you ever need, just call."

Ace focused on the road ahead. The only thing he needed was to pretend the feelings Randee awakened didn't exist. And the faster they got back to Omaha, the better. They'd go their separate ways, and he'd never have to see Randee again.

Randee pressed her fingers against her temples warding off the headache. A glance at the dashboard clock showed it was one o'clock in the morning. "Are we getting close to Randolph?"

"Yes."

"They should have burner cell phones or at least a landline," she said.

He shrugged. "Let's hope so."

The combination of snow-packed roads, balding tires and lack of weight in the truck's bed reduced their speed to a sloth's pace. Each passing minute elevated Randee's anxiety, but Ace drove with expert confidence even when the truck fishtailed on several icy patches.

Both remained quiet until he turned onto Highway 20 and a sign for the town of Randolph came into view. The orange-tinted ground reflected that the Department of Transportation had spread sand and begun clearing the roads.

Ace parked in front of the welcoming convenience store, and Randee unlatched her seat belt, too eager to contain her excitement. She was minutes from contacting her team. She hopped out of the truck before he shut off the engine.

"Wait up," Ace said, briefcase in hand.

She halted, though she longed to bolt ahead of him. At last, they entered together. The bell above the door chimed a greeting and the clerk—a man she'd guess to be in his sixties—leaned over the counter wearing a wide grin. "Ace Steele. Is that really you?"

Great. Reunion time.

Ace hesitated, and his shoulders visibly stiffened. Randee waited beside him, fighting the urge to yank him through the store. His demeanor gave her concern, and her hand instinctively went to the Glock resting in her hoodie pocket.

At last, Ace said, "Mr. Orfut, so nice to see you." He shifted the briefcase to his other hand. "Go ahead, hon."

Hon? She tried not to show her surprise at his choice of endearments as he gestured toward the inner part of the store. "I'll be just a minute. I need to catch up with Mr. Orfut. Oh, and would you grab a couple of coffees and something to munch on?"

Randee nodded dumbly as she grasped the briefcase handle. The men's conversation carried, and she monitored them while searching for burner phones.

Ace's jovial tone, though forced, sounded believable. They bounced around topics from the weather to the football season's best plays. Randee lost interest as she scanned the displays, locating the outdated flip phone. She grabbed the last remaining item and a portable car charger, then headed to the coffee machines.

The enormous glazed doughnuts reactivated her appetite, and she added two. Balancing her grocery items, she returned to where Ace still chatted it up with the older man at the counter.

"Sorry, hon." He helped her to unload everything as Orfut rang up the purchases.

"Yep, the missus makes these doughnuts." Orfut addressed her. Clearly, their departure wouldn't happen soon.

"They looked irresistible," she said.

He chuckled and lifted the cell phone, inspecting the device. "I didn't realize I had any of these in the store. Doesn't everyone use those smart kind now?"

Ace's plastered smile was almost comical. "If it was up to me, we'd all still have rotary phones."

Good diversion.

Orfut commented on every item, dragging the checkout procedure to twice the necessary time, then asked Randee, "So, where are you visiting us from?"

She glanced at Ace, and he responded with a small apologetic shrug. "Omaha. Guess I underestimated the storm." The weather was generally a safe subject.

"It is a mess out there, isn't it?" Orfut clucked his tongue as he rang up the car charger. "You folks would be wise to get off the roads. Just heard on the police scanner they found a body in the ditch near Highway 20. The poor soul was trying to drive a UTV out there. Who does that?"

Randee met Ace's eyes. "That's terrible." She lifted the bag and coffees while Ace paid.

He placed a hand on her back, signaling their departure. "Great seeing you, sir."

"You too, Ace. Don't be a stranger now." Orfut waved them off, and they scurried out of the store before the man cornered them in another long discussion.

Neither spoke until they'd both shut their doors and Ace had backed out of the parking space. Finally, Randee said, "Well, I guess we know what happened to our attacker." She withdrew a doughnut, passing it to him.

"Yeah." He shook his head.

"I thought we'd never get out of there, although I'm impressed at your improv conversation skills."

"I forgot Mr. Orfut and his wife recently bought the store. They're Hollow Hills's town gossips, more informative than the internet and newspapers combined. If Malte's men returned and stopped anywhere near my parents' home, I wanted to give them something to throw them off." He took a bite of the doughnut.

Randee opened the packaging and removed the phone. "Great thinking." She plugged the charger into the lighter, bringing the device to life.

"Told him you and I are headed up to Yankton, South Dakota, to meet with some of your old friends."

"And we're actually…"

"Going to Omaha. PrimeRight is closed for the weekend, and we can stay there until you decide what our next steps are."

Randee nodded. "That answer should come as soon as I make a call." She glanced at the display. No bars. Great.

"Once we get onto the highway, you should have some coverage."

Infusing her nervous energy into her doughnut, she munched in silence, monitoring the screen.

At last, service appeared, and she dialed Ishi's number, holding her breath. She answered on the second ring. "Hello?"

The sound of her friend's voice brought tears to Randee's eyes. "Ishi, it's Randee."

"Are you all right? Where are you? Do I need to send police your way?"

"We're headed back to Omaha from Randolph."

"What were you doing way out there?"

"Long story, but the weather is atrocious." Randee told Ishi about the intruder at Ace's parents' house. "We survived Malte's crew at the gala, but I lost communication with Sergio and Wesley."

"Somehow Malte's men interfered with the takedown. We're still not sure how. And someone planted a small bomb in the home office to break open the safe there."

Randee's mind whirled. "Was anyone hurt?"

"Fritz Nelson was taken to the hospital with injuries. I don't have any more information at this point. He was in the house at the time of the explosion. Thankfully, because of the fireworks, the partygoers were all outside, and the damage was restricted to the home office."

Randee considered the information. "Ace said Fritz told him to put Ghost in the safe during the party. He also said he had a huge surprise, which turned out to be fireworks."

"It's possible Malte and Nelson set up the fireworks to cover the explosion, allowing them access to the safe. Does Ace have the prototype?"

"Yes."

"Did he know about the fireworks?"

"No." Randee caught Ace's quizzical look in her peripheral vision.

"Has he tried to contact Fritz?"

"No." Ace hadn't had any opportunities to use the phone outside of her presence. Had he?

"Let's keep this short to prevent anyone from tapping into it. I'll text you a meeting location. Take care of you." She disconnected.

"I have to ask again. Who's Ishi?"

Randee focused on the road ahead. "She's a member of my team."

He flexed his jaw, and Randee sighed. "She'll contact us with the next steps." *Before I give up on this case.*

The engine's rumble provided background noise against the tension hanging between them.

"Orfut said the temperature is supposed to get up in the fifties by afternoon, so that should melt the snow."

How depressing that she'd pushed the poor scientist into discussing the weather. At least he was talking to her. "Gotta love Nebraska."

He chuckled, and it was sorely obvious how forced it was, but give the man an A for effort. Ace kept her on her toes with his unpredictable responses. He engaged in small talk, then seemed to emotionally distance himself when they neared anything personal.

"Can you dial a number for me?"

"Who—"

"I need to ask Mrs. O'Malley to take care of Rocko."

"It's really early morning or late depending on your point of view."

"She won't mind. She's an insomniac."

Sheepishly, she dialed and passed him the phone. "Sorry for calling at this hour, Mrs. O'Malley."

Ace's voice faded into the background as he requested the woman care for his cat. He ended the call and handed her back the phone.

Randee's mind raced through possibilities and consequences.

The burner phone buzzed, jolting her with a text message from Ishi's number.

Go straight to the abandoned farmhouse at Hwy 275 and 9. Bring Ghost and Steele. Take care of you.

"Thank You, Lord." Relief like fresh air infused energy back into her. "Great news! Ishi responded. We'll need to backtrack a little bit and head to the junction of Highway 275 and 9."

The nightmare was almost over, and she could return to her normal life.

TEN

The horror movie remnants of a house sent the tiny hairs on Randee's neck standing on end. Every dangling shingle and broken-out window of the decrepit box—leaning on what remained of its questionable foundation—told her to turn around and get out of there.

"Are you sure this is the place?" Ace drove through the long grove of overgrown trees and stopped beside the dilapidated two-story structure.

Randee studied the text message for the tenth time, confirming she hadn't misread the information. "It's not as if there's an abundance of abandoned properties on this road." A weak response to Ace's question. She surveyed the property again. "We did an op here several years ago. She probably chose it for that reason. A familiar place, you know?" And she'd justified her doubt.

He shifted into Park, leaving the engine running and highlights beaming on the house. "This is a bad idea."

She glared at him while silently agreeing with his concern. She'd been on enough covert operations to understand that sometimes it was better to go with the flow than ask a lot of questions. Ishi had a reason for sending them to this location, and she trusted her team. Didn't she? "Give it a minute. There's no point in a clandestine meeting if we advertise where we are. Turn off the headlights."

With a sigh, Ace complied. "Fine, but I'm not going to sit here and freeze. I'm leaving the engine running so we at least have heat."

"Okay." Randee twisted around, distracted and disappointed they were the first to arrive. Where was her team? She shifted in the seat and lifted the phone to call Ishi.

"Um, we have a problem."

"Hmm?" She didn't look up from dialing.

"Randee!"

She jerked at Ace's tone. Her attention turned to him, and she sucked in a breath at the small glowing red circle hovering over his heart. Her gaze traveled through the windshield in what felt like slow motion to the upper level of the dilapidated house and the sniper's hiding place.

"Get down." She grabbed his arm and tugged him sideways.

"Whatever happens, don't let them take Ghost." The man's life was in imminent danger and he was worried about the project?

The red light disappeared, replaced by the rumble of an engine and the approaching headlights. Randee slowly shifted and glanced at the rearview mirror.

A blacked-out van pulled up, blocking them in. Simultaneously, the burner phone rang from her fisted hand. Swallowing the dread that rose in her throat, she kept her eyes on Ace, willing him to stay perfectly still. "Hello?"

"Toss your gun out the window, or Mr. Steele is dead," the unfamiliar male voice ordered.

Without her weapon, how would she protect him?

"Do whatever they demand," Ace responded to her unspoken question.

"I'm tossing my gun." Randee manually rolled down

the window and threw out her weapon. "There," she said into the phone.

Two successive pops shifted the truck on flattened tires.

"Guess that eliminates our escape option," Ace grumbled.

"Good, send out Mr. Steele with the prototype," the man instructed.

"No. Let him go. I'll bring you the prototype," Randee contended.

"This isn't a negotiation!" The man spewed a series of earsplitting curses at a volatile rate.

Randee pulled the phone away from her ear, covering the speaker, and whispered to Ace, "Be ready to either fight or run."

He nodded.

The criminal stopped his childish rant and barked, "Do what you're told, now!"

"They want you to get out and bring Ghost," Randee said loudly for the caller's benefit, meeting Ace's wide eyes.

"Tell him to walk to the tailgate and set down the briefcase, then back away from it."

Randee repeated the order.

Ace cautiously lifted the case and pushed open the door. "Here goes nothing."

She watched, heart palpitating against her rib cage while her stomach bottomed out. This was it. They were going to die.

"Good, now join your friend. Slowly," the man ordered.

Randee exited the vehicle, careful to maintain an even pace while her mind sprinted through escape scenarios.

The van driver switched the headlights to high beams, blinding them. Randee shielded her face while trying to keep her attention on Ace, but the intensity made her eyes water.

The sound of footsteps from behind drew nearer, and Randee spun around, still unable to see past the spots dancing in front of her eyes. She gripped Ace's arm, his muscle tight under her hand. "Let's go."

"Don't even think about it." The lights dimmed, and the driver stepped onto the sideboard of the van, aiming his pistol at Ace.

Randee turned toward the footsteps, straining to focus, and spotted the man—presumably the sniper—approaching them. He stopped a short distance away, his automatic rifle trained and the red laser sight light on her heart.

"Toss your phone to me," the driver ordered, redirecting her attention.

Her eyes adjusted, and recognition dawned at the driver's familiar face. The man from the barn loft leaned against the door.

She glanced at the device in her hand, contemplating chucking the item at him. For Ace's sake, she complied, tossing it to the ground beside the van. The vehicle's illegally tinted windows prevented her from seeing inside. Not that it mattered. Whether there were two or twenty of Malte's goons, without a weapon, she had little or no hope of fighting them off. They could've just shot her and Ace with the scoped rifle, so what did they want?

The driver walked toward her wearing a smirk on his ugly mug and kicked the phone under the van. "You're fun to chase."

"Like deer hunting out of season." The other man chuckled.

Randee glared at the driver but remained silent.

His partner ordered, "Drop to your knees, hands behind your head."

She and Ace did as they were instructed while the driver scurried to collect the prototype.

"We got what we need. Let's finish them off," the criminal said.

"No, you know Malte's orders," he hissed, holding the briefcase with the delicacy of handling a live bomb. He hefted it toward the light and seemed to study the lock.

"Open it," his partner demanded.

"I can't. It's got some high-tech black square scanner thing," the driver advised.

"We'll just shoot it open."

"That won't work," Ace replied, his voice calm and confident.

"Yeah, and why not, Mr. Scientist?" the driver taunted.

"Because it's bulletproof, and any tampering with the lock will permanently disable the mechanism." Ace lifted his chin.

Randee scoured her brain. Was he speaking the truth? She didn't remember anything like that in the contract, but then her expertise wasn't in the technical issues. That was Ishi's realm.

"Then you're going to do it for us," his partner ordered.

"Are you sure Malte would be okay with you messing with his stuff?" Randee asked.

The men looked at each other as if considering her comment.

"She's right," the driver said, carrying the briefcase around to the back of the van.

The other man sighed. "You'd better be glad Malte wants you alive," he addressed Ace, then turned to Randee, gun raised. "However, we're allowed to kill you."

"Okay." She steadied her voice. "But you don't think the security of the briefcase would rely on just one man's authorization to open it, do you?" Realistically, they only needed Ace and the code, but she was desperate to keep them both alive.

"Is that so?" He chuckled.

A house divided cannot stand. The strange scripture popped into her mind, and she considered her present situation. They had to stay together. If the men separated them, they'd have no advantage.

The gunman seemed to chew on her words. Malte wouldn't have shared any pertinent details with them regarding the prototype. He was too much of a control freak. And the fact that he wanted Ace alive was good, ensuring they wouldn't kill him here. But Randee's life was inconsequential to them. She assessed the risk of attacking the gunmen.

Lord, what do I do?

"Like you said, Malte wants us alive, anyway," Randee interjected.

"No lady, he wants Steele alive," the driver corrected. "But we can always eliminate you once Malte gets what he wants."

The second man frowned, gun still trained on Randee and Ace. "Tie them up." He must be the leader of the two.

The driver scurried to the back of the van and returned carrying a roll of duct tape and no gun. He moved to Randee. "Put your hands together," he ordered.

She pretended to obey, determined not to make this easy for him. He leaned in and reached for her hands. At the same time, she thrust them upward, thumbs locked in a tight fist, and connected with his nose.

He fell back onto his behind, and she jumped up. Ace took the initiative and delivered several blows to the man's face. She dived for his partner's legs, tackling him to the ground, and the rifle skidded out of reach.

"Get the other gun," Randee hollered to Ace. The moment gave her assailant an opening, and he thrust a knee up, striking her in the chest and knocking the wind out of her. She flew back and landed with an *oomph*.

The man pushed himself up. "I don't need a gun to break your neck."

She jumped up to a fighting stance, hands outstretched and ready to attack. "You'll have to catch me first."

His rifle sat at a distance. Without it, he was a worthy opponent, but he also outweighed her. The gun was the advantage she needed. Randee faked him out by first moving to the right, then launching herself toward the rifle on the left. But he caught her midflight, strangling her legs.

She braced for the fall and landed hard on her face. His powerful grip dragged her backward as she clawed at the snow and dirt, straining to reach the weapon. The man's hold was too strong. He whipped her along the wet ground, then flipped her over onto her back, pinning her arms down under his knees. "Be still or I'll knock you out."

She struggled, then realized there were no other sounds coming from where Ace had fought with the driver.

In answer to her silent question, the driver rushed to his partner's side, gun clearly visible. "That was fun," he huffed, yanking Randee to her feet.

He gripped her arm painfully tight and hoisted her by her biceps, forcing Randee to stand on tiptoe to avoid having her arm ripped out of the socket. Her eyes scanned the area. No sign of Ace. Panic outweighed her pain. Where was he?

The driver tossed his partner the roll of duct tape, and he bound her wrists behind her back. Randee didn't fight him off, her concern for Ace overriding the struggle. "Where's Ace?"

"I took care of him." He hefted the rifle and handed it to his partner.

Randee swallowed. Had he killed Ace? She tugged against his hold, which caused him to laugh. "Where is he? What did you do?"

"You're a feisty little thing, aren't you?" he said, moving behind her. "Let's go."

Randee lifted her foot and delivered a hard kick to the man's knee.

He hollered, stumbling, then retaliated with a sudden thrust, striking her on the temple with the butt of the gun. Stunned, she dropped to her knees. He hovered over her, a murderous glare on his face. "Get up."

She complied, and the driver dragged her to the rear of the van where Ace lay sprawled on the ground, unconscious, beside the tires.

"Is he—" She couldn't bear to speak the last word.

"Dead? No." The driver swiped at his bleeding nose.

Relief flooded her. But with Ace knocked out, there was no way they'd escape the men. Her captor shoved her inside the empty van, and she landed knee-first on the cold steel. She inched to a sitting position and backed against the wall, assessing the structure.

The men hefted Ace, tossed him carelessly on the cold floor and slammed the doors. Randee awkwardly shuffled to his side, but with her hands behind her back, she couldn't even check his pulse. She leaned over, feeling the heat from his breath against her cheek. *Thank You, Lord.*

The overhead light came on as the men entered the vehicle on opposite sides. She surveyed her surroundings, spotting the briefcase on the floorboards up front.

Out of reach.

The van lurched forward, and she wavered off-balance, drawing her knees closer to her chest.

Oh Lord, what do I do now?

ELEVEN

"Ace!" The warm whisper tickled his ear, but the rough nudge to his side forced him awake.

Loud, raucous electric guitars screamed, and the deafening double-bass drum solo added to the impact wrench pelting the inside of his skull. He squeezed his eyes shut to combat the wretched music reverberating around him. His body unwillingly swayed with the subsequent rocking of the ground beneath him. His stomach roiled in a nauseating twist, and Ace rolled to his side.

"Ace!" the voice urged again.

He blinked, adjusting to the dim light, and spotted Randee squatting beside him. Concern etched deep lines across her forehead. "Thank God." Her words were drowned out by the obnoxious raging from the speakers.

Ace surveyed the space. His back was against the single bench seat separating them from where the driver and passenger belted along to the blaring music in a horrendous lack of melody. "Where are we?" he asked, doubtful she heard him.

She gave a jerk of her head and sat up straighter, her focus fixed on the men.

Ace followed her gaze.

Was he visible in the rearview mirror? How long had he been out?

The song ended, and the driver spoke. "Is Sleeping Beauty awake?"

Ace closed his eyes and remained motionless. Better if they believed he was unconscious.

A pause, movement in front, accompanied by a cackle. "Nope, he's still out."

The man must've had to peer over the seat to check on him. Good. That provided Ace a small advantage. He gritted his teeth, fixated on Randee. A new rendition of blaring music and caterwauling consumed the space.

Randee's posture relaxed slightly, and she nodded as if assuring him it was safe. Her focus returned to the men, and Ace attempted to sit up, realizing his hands were bound behind him. He wriggled with the movement of the van, tugging hard against the restraints.

A sudden jolt of the van's tires in what he assumed to be a pothole provided Ace the necessary resistance. The ties broke apart, and the remnants clung to his wrists.

He brought his arms around front and inadvertently brushed Randee's leg, eliciting a fragment of a twitch. Her face was frozen in a stoic blank expression. She gave a marginal twist, giving him a view of her hands bound behind her back.

Why had the kidnappers used a zip tie on him and duct tape on her? Easier to remove, but how would he do that without drawing their attention?

Ace remained lying down and rolled to the other side, facing the front of the van. Movement caught his eye. A long cylinder rocked beneath the bench seat. A crowbar!

He slid the weapon out slowly using the music's crescendo as cover. Crowbar gripped in his palm, he gestured to Randee.

She responded with a quick nod, then inched closer and twisted, allowing him access to her hands. He bit into the tape and tore a small section. She did the rest, removing the binding with fluid motion so not to attract the kidnappers' unwanted attention.

Randee pointed low at the driver, and Ace nodded understanding, then passed her the crowbar.

"Watch out for that deer!" she hollered.

The driver slammed on the brakes.

Ace braced himself from hitting the back of the seat.

"What deer?" the passenger barked.

"Sorry, thought it was an animal crossing the road," Randee said, with a shrug.

"Maybe we need to gag her and keep her quiet." The driver accelerated.

Ace shifted to a squat, and Randee mouthed, "One, two—"

On three, they attacked.

He threaded his hands through the driver's greasy long hair and slammed his head into the steering wheel. The knockout worked, and the man slumped over.

A sickening thud next to him confirmed Randee had accomplished the same with the passenger and crowbar.

Ace lunged over the headrest and grasped the wheel, battling for control. The van swerved and continued speeding with the driver's foot lodged against the accelerator.

"Get him out of the way," Ace hollered.

Randee grabbed the man's torso, but his massive size and dead weight prevented her from doing more than forcing him onto his side. Ace climbed over the seat but wasn't able to access the steering wheel or pedals.

"Grab the wheel," he ordered.

Randee moved behind him and steered while Ace shoved the driver against the unconscious passenger.

She screamed as the van plummeted into a ditch. Ace

quickly slid over to the driver's side and resumed control, bounding back onto the road.

Ace slammed on the brakes, bringing the vehicle to an abrupt halt. His pulse raged, and his breath came out in quick gasps. He shifted into Park and turned off the obnoxious music. "Are you okay?"

Randee leaned over the seat inches from his cheek. Their eyes met, and his heart did a triple beat. Whether from exertion or the nearness of her, he wasn't sure. Neither looked away until the driver groaned.

"Looks like our dozing kidnappers are coming to. We'd better move fast." Ace climbed out and sprinted to the rear doors, yanked them open and assisted Randee.

"Great job, by the way." She slapped his back a little harder than he'd anticipated.

"Not too bad yourself." He grinned, adrenaline still rushing through him.

She reached into the van and produced a roll of duct tape. Together, they dragged each man to the ground, placing them on their stomachs. Ace bound the men's arms and ankles behind their backs, finishing with tape over their mouths. "Do you think they have a phone?"

"Let's hope." Randee checked the assailants' pockets and withdrew a burner phone with a dead battery. "Guess that's not going to help." She threw it on the ground. "Doubtful it can be traced, but we don't want Malte's men tracking us. We need to get to civilization and ditch this van."

"What about our friends here?" Ace gestured toward the men.

"It's too cold to leave them out here. Let's put them in the back of the van and the cops can deal with them."

"Works for me."

They hoisted the men into the vehicle, then climbed in. Randee pulled the criminals' guns out from the floorboard. Ace double-checked the briefcase, ensuring everything was safe.

"Have any idea where we are?" he asked.

"Not really. I couldn't see much from back there. We made several turns, and you were out for eight of those horrible songs. Roughly thirty minutes."

Ace shifted into gear, and they drove on in silence. Randee hovered over the seat, keeping a watch on the unconscious men.

Finally, the dim lights of a service station loomed ahead. Ace accelerated, anxious to reach the place. But as they neared, his hopes were dashed; it was doubtful the tiny business sold cell phones.

He traded his wallet for the gun. "I'll keep an eye on our friends."

Randee nodded and slipped out.

She hurried into the store, and his gaze bounced between her and the service attendant. The frown on her face as she returned said the news wasn't good. "He didn't have any phones, but he said there's another station just four miles east of here."

"And where is here?"

"Decatur."

They were much farther north than he'd anticipated, so they'd have to drive south to get to Omaha.

He gripped the steering wheel tighter. "Is your team—"

"Everything has been compromised. If Malte tampered with Ishi's secure line, I'm not sure what to do."

Ace had no one else to call. Even if Fritz had survived the explosion, he wasn't capable of protecting them from Malte. Yolanda had her son to consider. Ace wouldn't put either of them in more danger.

His hopes were dashed when he pulled up to the second station, with a single gas pump and almost nothing of a store. He shifted into Park, keeping an eye on the rearview mirror and the men in the back. They'd survived so much together, and although she'd withheld details, she'd also risked her life on multiple occasions. His frustration melted. "Randee, I trust your judgment."

The words seemed to overwhelm her, and he caught a brief quiver of her lower lip as her expression softened. "Thank you," she whispered.

He squeezed her shoulder in what he hoped wasn't too forward a move. She smiled and laid her hand over his, calming his worries. They stayed that way for several seconds. With a jerk, she moved out from under his touch, a grin spreading across her face. "There's one other person who might be able to help us."

"Okay."

"My ATF mentor, Elias Archer. He'll know what to do." She climbed out of the van and rushed into the store.

Ace withheld his concern that another ATF contact didn't register high on his confidence and assurance list. Except he'd just told Randee he trusted her. And he meant it. She was the expert between them. Yet he couldn't shake the feeling that involving more ATF agents was a mistake. It would be so much easier to go to the authorities. Why wasn't she willing to do that? He shook off the worry. She had a job to do. He might not agree with the methods, but he refused to add to her already-heavy burdens.

If this contact turned out to be involved with more of Malte's men, he was done. He'd go to the police himself and bear her disdain. Satisfied with his backup plan and the small portion of control—however fleeting it might be— he focused on Randee talking to the young male attendant.

The slight shake of the guy's head sent a wave of worry through Ace. Without a phone, what did they do?

The muffled groan from behind him had Ace swiveling around, gun at the ready.

* * *

"Are you okay, lady?"

Randee guessed the young man's age to be nineteen or twenty. Legally able to work an overnight shift but possessing so many boyish qualities.

Lady. At least he was polite. "I've had one of those everything-that-could-go-wrong-does kind of days."

He snorted. "Right? Sounds like my night. First, I get this text from my girlfriend. She's all mad because I have to be here. I tried telling her—"

Randee gripped the counter, steadying herself, and forced a calm she didn't feel into her voice. "I'm sorry, don't mean to cut you off, but I really need to make a call. May I use your landline?"

"Landline?" He blinked as though she'd spoken in a foreign language.

"The phone with a cord attached to the wall?" Trying to get him to maintain eye contact for more than ten seconds at a time was wearing her out. They'd already established the store didn't sell burner phones, and she was about to snatch the barely-over-eighteen's cell out of his hands.

He laughed. "Is that what those dinosaurs are called?"

"Yes, do you have one here?"

"Back in the office." He reverted to his text messaging.

A moment of alarm had Randee reconsidering the offer. She looked out the shop window hoping to make eye contact with Ace, but he was twisted around focused on the assailants.

They needed help now, and she had one option. With resignation, she released her hold on the counter. "Thank you." She rushed to the office, pausing at the partly open door. A small metal sign warned Authorized Personnel Only.

Randee reached for the light switch, illuminating the tiny space and wall-to-wall desk. She spotted the once-ivory phone, covered in black fingerprints, and lifted the receiver, praying she remembered the number. It had been so long since she'd spoken to her mentor. A glance at the ticking clock indicated it was after two o'clock. She cringed and dialed.

Elias Archer's unmistakable gruff voice brought immediate comfort. "Do you have any idea what time it is?"

"I'm sorry, Elias, but this is an emergency."

"Miranda? Is that you?" His tone softened.

"Yes, sir, and I need your help."

"What's wrong? Where are you? Are you okay?"

She smiled at his snarly exterior melting into concern. "Yes, for now. But could you give me a ride?"

"Already headed out the door. Where are you?"

"Four miles south of Decatur at the Gas N'Up Station." She searched the desk, found a bill with the service station's address and repeated it to Elias.

"I'll push every speed limit, but I'm talking on my hands-free device. So tell me what's going on."

Randee spilled everything about the explosion, Malte's attacks and the present situation where the kidnappers lay unconscious in the van with Ace keeping watch.

"You're on active assignment?"

"That's just it, I don't know. I can't reach Ishi, Sergio or Wesley. Malte somehow compromised Ishi's secure line. I'm at a loss." Randee sank into the chair, anxious to get back to Ace but desperate for Elias's wisdom.

"I'll make some calls and see what I can find out. In the meantime, do you have a weapon?"

"They made me toss my Glock, but we have their guns."

"Good. Keep them bound and out of sight until I get there. Then we'll call the local PD and give them the arrest."

"Yes, sir."

"Stop with the 'sir,' Miranda. We're way past that."

She grinned. "Right."

"How long before the men come to?"

Randee smiled. "Let's just say even when they do, they'll be quiet."

He grunted again. "Park around the back of the building. I'll be there as soon as I can." He disconnected.

Randee exited the office, feeling better than she had in ages. "Thank you."

The attendant gave her a second glance before returning to his phone. "Yeah, sure."

"Take her flowers. A sweet gesture does wonders."

That got his attention. He met her eyes. "Really?"

"Roses if possible," she said, smiling.

"Right." He sighed.

"We've had a bad night. Would you mind if we parked around the back of the building and slept a little while we wait for our ride to show up?"

His phone chimed, and he shrugged, offering a distracted, "Whatever works for you."

Ace looked visibly relieved at her return to the van. "I debated leaving our sleeping pals to check on you." He passed her the gun and pulled on his seat belt. "Where to?"

"Actually, we're going to hang here for a bit. Elias is on his way, so he suggested parking around back until he arrives."

"How long?"

"A little over an hour. We are in the middle of nowhere."

He frowned. "But shouldn't we drive to meet him? Cut the time in half?"

"No, we can take turns catnapping and keeping watch on our friends."

Ace shook his head and pulled around to the rear of the store. He shut off the engine. "I'll stay up with them."

"No, I can—"

"Randee, how much sleep have you had in the past two days?"

She grimaced. "A little."

"Then let me take the first watch and you nap. What kind of vehicle am I looking for?"

"Probably an SUV, dark colored. That would be Elias's style."

"Okay, I'll wake you when he gets here."

"I don't need long, a few minutes max."

"Sleep. I've got this."

She tugged her hoodie tighter, enjoying the idea of someone taking care of her. "Should we leave the van running?"

"For over an hour? No. Here, lean on me."

Randee scooted closer and relaxed against his chest, stretching her legs across the seat. He adjusted with his back to the door, keeping the kidnappers in view, gun in hand.

The soft *thump* of his heartbeat and rhythmic breathing calmed her. Maybe it was the sheer exhaustion of being awake and on the run for two days. Or the fact that help was coming. Whatever the reasoning, Randee allowed herself to close her eyes. Just a few minutes was all she needed.

"Randee." The deep rumble interacted with her dream. "Wake up."

She bolted upright and pressed herself against the door, heart pounding a hundred miles an hour.

Ace held up a hand, the other gripping the gun. "Relax. Your friend is here."

Randee blinked to clear her vision and absorb Ace's words. "How…how long—" Her mouth was dry, making speech difficult.

"About forty-five minutes. You were out." Ace gave her a boyish grin. "And you talk in your sleep."

Heat rose in her cheeks. No. What had she said?

He must've sensed her fear because he blurted, "No worries, most of it was unintelligible, except for my name."

Great. That was even worse.

Thankfully, the bound men interrupted the conversation, grousing with their restraints. Randee turned to them. "Calm down, that tape will be coming off in a jiffy. Of course, it'll be exchanged for handcuffs. You might want to quit complaining. PD should be here soon."

The men's eyes widened, and both went still.

"Are you okay to sit with them while I talk to Elias?" She gripped the door handle, desperate to escape the confines with Ace before she learned more about her embarrassing antics.

"Absolutely. Just make sure he's legit first. If something's wrong give me a signal."

"Like what?"

"Scream."

"That'd be subtle." She climbed out.

Elias parked his brand-new SUV beside them, and the sight of his familiar face was a balm to her stressed soul. He was out of his vehicle and tugging her into a hug in seconds. "Hey, kid, you look the worse for wear."

"Thanks." She stepped back and tucked her hands into her hoodie pocket.

"Let's get you someplace safe."

"That would be fabulous. But what about Malte's goons?"

"Already called the PD. They'll be here in a few minutes, so we need to boogie before they show up and save ourselves a lot of explaining."

"Perfect." She rushed to Ace. "Let's roll."

He passed her the briefcase, then, carrying the gun and keys, joined her in front of the van. "We should prevent them from following us. Give me a second."

"Make it fast," Elias said.

Ace shot him a hard look, handed the items to Randee and popped the van's hood.

"What are you doing?" she asked, arms full with the equipment.

"Repaying the favor their buddy left for us at the house."

"Great thinking." She walked to Elias's vehicle and placed everything on the back seat, then climbed in.

"What is he doing?" Elias asked.

Randee explained how the intruder at the ranch had disabled their truck. Ace was doing the same, in case the men escaped their bindings.

Within a few minutes, Ace shut the hood and pulled open the passenger door.

"You get shotgun," she said smiling.

He grinned. "Thanks."

"So, what did you do to the van?" Elias asked.

Ace held up a red wire with small black tips that Randee didn't recognize. "Removed the coil wire."

Once they reached the road, the blare of sirens confirmed the local PD was on the way. "Malte's men are going to jail," Elias assured them.

"Excellent. Is it okay if we stay at your house until I can get more information?" Randee leaned forward.

"Of course," Elias said.

"How long do you anticipate we'll be gone?" Ace asked.

"Depends. I've got calls in to a few connections, and I'm waiting to hear back." Elias glanced at her in the rearview mirror, a questioning expression in his eyes.

Ace sighed. "Guess Rocko will have to do without me for a little longer."

"Who?"

Randee grinned. "His cat."

Elias nodded. "How a man cares for his animals says a lot about his character."

She couldn't have said it better herself.

TWELVE

Randee padded barefoot down the dark hallway and paused briefly at the resounding snore emanating from beneath Ace's closed bedroom door. He'd dozed off repeatedly in a pathetic effort to stay awake on the ride to the house. Elias had ordered the scientist straight to bed immediately upon their arrival. To his credit, Ace hadn't put up much of a struggle.

A grin played on her lips. At least one of them was recouping sleep.

Not for lack of trying, but Randee's racing thoughts had other intentions. After two hours of flopping back and forth like a fish on land and staring at the ceiling fan, she'd given up.

She gripped the handrail and slipped quietly down the stairs to the main floor, then aimed for the kitchen. Elias's minimalistic and obsessively clean lifestyle made her search for a mug relatively easy. Perusing the variety of hot drink mini plastic pod options encased in the spinning rack, she finally selected decaf coffee, inserting it into the single-serving machine. While waiting for the brew, Randee leaned against the counter, reveling in the familiar comfort of the spotless kitchen.

She moved to the sliding glass doors and gazed out into

the darkness. The modest house consisted of two levels and a fully finished walkout basement centered on acreage outside of Omaha. Randee thought Elias would move after his wife, Ursula, passed away. He'd adamantly stated his preference for privacy and solace—even if it required a longer commute—over the confines of too-close nosy neighbors.

Randee sensed movement behind her and twisted around, instinctively grasping the Glock hidden in her hoodie pocket.

Vasili, Elias's gray Persian cat, approached, tail swaying.

Randee heaved a sigh of relief and dropped her gun into her pocket. "You startled me, boy."

The overweight feline rubbed against her legs with a purred demand for a dose of affection. She knelt and stroked his feathery fur. When her coffee finished, Vasili meowed disapproval at the withdrawal of her touch.

Randee retrieved the steaming mug, and Vasili fell in step beside her as she walked toward the soft glow exuding from Elias's office at the far end of the home. The low rumble of her mentor's hushed voice slowed her stride.

She halted near the ajar door, unwilling to stop her shameless eavesdropping, and strained to hear him. Randee homed in on partial sentences that included words like *missing*, *undetermined* and *hostage*.

Vasili pushed his way into the room, blowing her cover. *So much for that idea.* She sighed and rapped softly before entering. Elias waved her inside, then concluded his phone call.

"Why aren't you sleeping?"

She leaned against the door frame. "I tried, but my brain wouldn't shut off. Why are you awake?"

"Making some calls."

Vasili crossed the room, jumped onto the desk and sprawled on his side.

"At this time of night?" She glanced at the brass clock on the wall. Six o'clock. "Or morning, rather."

Elias snorted. "Law enforcement doesn't have business hours, Miranda. I assume Steele is still sawing logs?"

Randee looked behind her, then back at her mentor, curiosity building at his question. "Based on the snoring from his room, yes."

"Good." Elias steepled his fingers on the spotless cherrywood desk. "Please shut the door. If his surreptitious snooping skills are better than yours, I don't want him to overhear us talking."

She winced, ears burning with embarrassment. Without a word, she plodded to the chair opposite Elias and slid onto the soft leather seat, cradling her cup. "I take it you don't have good news for me."

Elias had aged since his retirement from the ATF. The deep lines around his blue-green irises conveyed years of wisdom and his propensity to laugh. But at this hour, even his full graying beard didn't hide his downcast expression.

"I wish I could downplay your worry, but I can't." He sat up straighter, meeting her eyes with an intensity that plunged like a stone to the pit of her stomach.

"What's going on?" She swallowed hard.

"Wesley Zimmer and Sergio Vargas have been missing since the party. It's believed they were taken hostage by Malte's men."

"Hostage?" The word sucked the breath from her lungs. "No. They can't be. Ishi never said anything about that when I talked to her." The hot cup seared her hands, but Randee continued to grip the mug. The discomfort ensured she wasn't dreaming. "I never should've—"

"Listen up, kid." The seriousness of Elias's tone kept her from continuing her sentence. "Did you or did you not tell me Vargas ordered you to leave with Steele and the prototype?"

She nodded numbly, drowning in the news, and refused to look up. He didn't understand. She'd abandoned her team, left them in danger or worse. If Malte had them, they were dead. There was no justification sufficient to alleviate the guilt.

"Miranda, you did your job, and sometimes that means doing the hard stuff. If Vargas wanted your assistance, he would've said so. It wasn't a matter of pride. He knew the mission, and you need to remember it, too."

"Yes, sir." She took a sip of coffee, forcing down the boulder lodged in her throat, and met the compassion in Elias's eyes.

They had to be alive. Focus on the positive. "Do you have an update on Fritz Nelson's condition? Is Yolanda Ruiz okay?"

Elias grimaced. "Apparently, Fritz was in the house when the small device on the safe detonated. He's alive, but my source said he hasn't regained consciousness. Ruiz remains beside him, keeping vigil."

She nodded, relieved both parties were safe. "That sounds like Yolanda. She's a thoughtful, sweet lady." Randee's eyes welled with tears, and she blinked them away. Crying meant defeat, and until they knew for sure about Sergio's and Wesley's status, she wouldn't surrender.

"I need you to put on your investigator hat. Have you considered the possibility that Steele was in on the raid?"

She jerked up and shook her head.

Elias lifted his hand, stilling her. "Listen to me. He had to have known about the fireworks being used to cover the sound of the device opening the safe. He escaped in the nick of time with the prototype. Maybe he's working both sides looking for the biggest payout."

No. Ace wouldn't. Couldn't. "We were both in danger."

"Are you sure?"

The men had burst through, demanding Ace. Hadn't they? "But he helped me to escape, too."

"Were you with him in the house the entire time?"

Randee recalled losing Steele in the busyness of the gala. He'd looked surprised when she barged in on him while he was removing Ghost from the safe. Neither had expected the other to show up. Doubt clung to her mind, a complicated spiderweb expanding with each connecting thought. Worse, she couldn't dispute Elias's concerns.

"Your lack of response tells me you're chewing on what I've said. Good, because we have some things to address regarding Steele."

That got her full attention. "Like?"

"Are you aware the evidence implicates him as the only developer—"

She shook her head. "That's part of his contract. He was assigned to build Ghost."

Elias quirked a disapproving eyebrow at her interruption. "Vargas's records implicate Ace as the spy communicating with Malte."

Randee jumped up so fast she spilled the hot coffee on her hand and leg. "No. That's impossible. Sergio would've told me."

Elias tossed her a tissue from the box on his desk to mop up the mess. "Sounds to me like you've lost your objectiveness regarding Steele."

"I'm not… I—"

"Miranda, you're defending the man before I even finish telling you what I know."

Randee bit her lip. "I'm sorry."

Elias stood and rounded the desk, perching on the edge. "Hey, I understand the difficulty in keeping an emotional distance. It's one of the dangers of working undercover. Haven't I warned you about that in the past?"

"Yes, sir." She dropped back onto the seat.

"In order to maintain your cover and properly work the case, you must remain objective. That means considering all the evidence, which includes the reality that Ace Steele has the most to gain by working with Malte."

Randee hated his words.

Hated that everything he said made sense, and she couldn't refute his accusation with facts.

Hated that a tiny prick of doubt penetrated her professional armor.

She delayed her response by taking another sip, but buying time didn't work, and she still came up empty.

"Your best course of action is to finish this assignment. If Vargas's intel is wrong, you'll exonerate Steele with evidence."

And if not, she'd be forced to arrest and charge Ace with treason while wearing his deceased sister's clothing. "What if—"

Her mentor's unyielding gaze prodded her to continue.

She hesitated. Her spoken thoughts would be a betrayal against her team. Against the ATF. Except Elias was her deepest confidant and at this point, the only person she trusted entirely. "Hear me out."

"I'm listening."

"When I called Ishi for help, Malte's men showed up. You don't think—"

"What?" He folded his arms across his chest, and skepticism tainted his tone.

"It sounds ludicrous, but isn't it feasible that Ishi, Sergio and Wesley are also working for Malte? They'd have every opportunity to frame Ace to take the fall once they obtained Ghost. If Ace intended to sell Ghost to the highest bidder, he could've taken off any time before this. My team is waiting for the delivery of the completed prototype. Every attack has focused on stealing the prototype."

Elias exhaled. "Good point. I can't argue in your team's defense. Thirty-five years in law enforcement taught me anything is possible when it comes to criminal activity. Seems to me, your only hope is to uncover the spy. But Miranda—"

She gave him her unwavering focus.

"—you must hide your emotions. Handle the case with facts and nothing else. Your feeling, gut, instinct, whatever you want to call it, is deceptive. We see what we want to see. Hear what we want to hear. The heart is deceitful above all things."

Randee leaned forward, her elbows resting on her knees. "Then how do you know who to trust?"

"You trust God and let Him guide you, while acknowledging what will break your heart. Because kid, in your case, it might save your life."

The next morning, Ace awoke with one motivating thought: they couldn't run forever. Once Malte caught them—as he no doubt eventually would—Ghost would be compromised.

With the briefcase tucked in the crook of his arm, Ace crept into the bathroom and locked the door. He opened the medicine cabinet, removed a roll of athletic tape and an elastic bandage, then went to work wrapping the plans and Ghost. He secured the package to the underside of the toilet tank lid with the tape. *Please don't let them fall.*

He took the empty briefcase back to the bedroom where the morning sun beamed brightly through the open blinds, casting its warmth and promise of a new day. Ace laid on the freshly made bed and stared at the ceiling.

Two swift knocks jolted him upright. Heart stampeding like a herd of elephants, he pushed up and opened the door.

Elias Archer stood in the entry in a confrontational stance, his lips thinned in a no-nonsense expression. "I hope I didn't wake you."

"No, sir." The man's intimidating presence filled the space, and he didn't move. Everything in his demeanor dripped of disdain.

One stride forward brought him inches from Ace's chin. Although Ace stood a foot taller, and he was more than two decades younger than Elias, Ace had no doubt regarding the man's physical agility. Still, he didn't back down or cower.

Elias lowered his voice. "Are you the man Miranda believes you to be?"

Ace swallowed. "I beg your pardon?"

"If you care about her at all, do the right thing. For once in your life." He did an about-face and spoke louder. "Mr. Steele, please join Miranda and me downstairs."

What was that all about? "Yes, sir." Ace turned and grabbed the briefcase—now light without the prototype and heavy with his apprehension for hiding it—and followed Elias down the steps.

Randee glanced up as they entered the kitchen. "Morning." Her tone was flat, uninviting, and the dark circles under her eyes said she hadn't rested. "Coffee?"

"Yes, please." He stood awkwardly beside the counter.

She gestured toward a rack of K-Cups. "Any preference?"

"The highest octane you've got." Though he'd slept well, it hadn't been a rejuvenating sleep. Worry had wrestled his stomach into knots and the improv tête-à-tête wasn't helping.

"Coming up," she said a little too cheerfully.

"Have a seat. I'll be right back." Elias exited, Vasili trailing behind.

"What's going on?" Ace whispered as he moved to the kitchen table.

She joined him and glanced at the doorway. "I'm not entirely sure. Elias said we need to talk."

"What's his problem with me?"

Elias returned, squelching the conversation with his obvious displeasure lingering thick in the atmosphere. Randee gave Ace a single shoulder shrug and served mugs of coffee.

"Sorry to wake you with bad news, but there isn't time to dance around the problem."

Ace looked at Randee, unsure which problem Elias referred to.

Elias addressed Randee. "First, I've spoken with Ishi, and she has requested a meeting alone with you, Miranda. She'd like for you to bring Ghost. However, there's a complication that will require you to meet her in an undisclosed location."

"What kind of complication?" Randee asked.

"You and Ace are named as persons of interest, and you're wanted for questioning in the disappearance of Wesley Zimmer and Sergio Vargas. As well as the incident that put Fritz Nelson in the hospital." Elias leaned forward, daring Ace to argue with his penetrating gaze.

"What?" Ace pushed back from the table, splashing coffee onto the oak surface.

Randee snatched a kitchen towel and quickly absorbed the liquid. She leaned against the counter wringing her hands. "Both of us?"

"There's an eyewitness claiming he overheard you conspiring prior to the explosion in the home office." Elias's even tone held no variation, as if he were reporting the weather forecast.

"Malte," Randee said, shaking her head.

"Most likely. If he can't get to you with his cronies, he'll use the authorities to draw you in. If you refuse to comply, a warrant will be issued for your arrest." Elias addressed Randee, leaving the distinct impression he'd prefer Ace weren't in the room. "Miranda, your career is on the line. If you stay in hiding, you'll look guilty."

She blinked. "I'm undercover. The ATF—"

"—won't release anything if it'll blow the case. You know that. The other option to going alone and meeting Ishi is to leave the prototype with me and I'll make the transfer."

Ace stared down at his hands, recalling the hidden prototype in the upstairs bathroom. *Should I tell them?* He glanced up and met Elias's narrowed gaze. Randee might trust him, but Ace didn't. *No. Not yet.* And the man's command pierced Ace's guilt in the jugular. *Do the right thing for once.*

He worked his jaw. Turning himself in was the only way to protect Randee. Besides, he had nothing to hide. And at least in police custody, he'd be safe. Hopefully.

"Take me in." The words escaped his mouth before Ace gave them full consent. There was no taking them back.

Randee jerked to look at him, an incredulous frown on her face. "Why would you want to do that?"

"Because we both know Malte's never going to stop. How long are we supposed to hide?"

She shook her head. "No, we can't compromise the case by telling the PD about Ghost."

"That's a good idea. And leave the briefcase here with

me and Randee." Elias planted both hands flat on the table. "She'll get it to the ATF."

Or you'd steal it. If Elias planned to take Ghost and sell it, Randee remained in danger. Elias must believe Ace possessed the prototype in the empty briefcase, and the assumption kept the bull's-eye on him, where it belonged.

Ace shook his head and worked to keep his tone even, assured of his decision to maintain Ghost's secret hiding place. "That won't be necessary. Think about it. In the end, you know it's me they really want." He continued, "It's my integrity the authorities doubt. If the press paints me as a criminal, that's what people will believe. I won't drag you down with me. You have everything to lose. What do I have left except for the prototype?"

"Ace." Compassion swam in Randee's eyes.

"You'd take possession of it. It belongs to the ATF, anyway."

She seemed to consider that, and a shadow passed over her face. "Even if you surrendered, Malte wouldn't stop. He'd have you right where he wants you. Owning Ghost isn't enough. He wants the ability to reproduce the prototype for his legion of militia followers. He's got people everywhere, including jail. You won't be protected there."

"Again, which is why Ghost should remain here," Elias interrupted.

"The guards—" Ace argued.

"—many of them are on Malte's payroll. No, it's not an option." Randee slapped the towel on the counter.

A small bubble of relief entered his heart, burst immediately by Elias's response. "Listen to Steele. He should surrender while you continue working the case."

Ace groaned inwardly. *Sure, now you're telling her to believe me.*

"That's settled. I'll contact Ishi with the arrangements," Elias said.

"No. I'll contact her," Randee interjected.

Elias frowned. "Very well. You have a lot to talk about before we take you in, Ace. I haven't slept all night, and I'm too old to be pulling all-nighters. I'm going to lie down. Wake me when you decide how you want to proceed. In the meantime, you're safe here."

"That's debatable," Ace argued.

Elias's jaw went taut. "Steele, we don't know each other very well, so I'll pretend not to be offended by your comment. But rest assured, when I give my word on something, I'm confident in the end result." With that, he exited the kitchen.

Once his footfalls moved up the stairs, Ace spoke. "What was that all about?"

"Elias doesn't like being questioned."

"What do you think about leaving Ghost here?"

Randee regarded him. "That's not a bad idea. This is our one safe place, and Elias would never put me in danger."

"Yeah, but he'd toss me in front of a firing squad."

She shrugged. "His delivery is just a little rough."

Ace snorted. "No offense, Randee, but all the faith you've had in your circle of people seems misplaced. We trusted Ishi, and Malte ambushed us. What happens when Malte finds us here?"

"He won't. You heard Elias. I'm not arresting you. We'll figure this out."

"Okay, then agree that we're on our own. We can't depend on anyone else."

She pursed her lips, and something akin to suspicion moved in her blue eyes.

Ace continued, "You violated the contract by telling Elias about Ghost."

She glanced down, turning her coffee cup in her hands. "I can't argue there. But Elias isn't dirty. He's the only person I trust completely."

Ace forced himself to remain aloof, soaking in Randee's biting comment. The *only* person she trusted? The words concreted Ace in his place.

Randee seemed oblivious to his affront and continued, "He's more than a mentor. He's the closest family member I have. Elias took me under his wing after my father—"

Ace contemplated whether to pry, but the glimpse into her personal life piqued his curiosity. "May I ask what happened to your father?"

Randee's lip trembled slightly, but she recovered her composure and sat up straighter. "He was killed when his alias was blown in an undercover ATF operation."

Ace leaned back, absorbing the information. "I'm so sorry for your loss. So, it's just you and your mother?"

Randee released a bark of a laugh. "Sort of. She basically disowned me when I refused to quit."

Unsure how to respond, he didn't.

She sighed. "My mother hated everything about the ATF. My father spent most of his career in undercover roles that often took him away for extended periods of time. She never understood his commitment to the job. Instead, she viewed his strong work ethic as a competition. She believed he preferred any assignment that kept him from her. Thing was, my father was an awesome agent. Smart. Quick on his feet. He was a chameleon, blending in perfectly to every case. Until one of the men he convicted discovered his true identity. Word got back to the criminals he was gathering evidence on, and they killed him." Her shoulders slumped as if the reminder weighed anew on her.

"Is that why you became an agent?"

Randee sipped her coffee. "I admired my father. He was

always teaching me something. I wanted to be just like him."
The sorrow in her eyes shimmered with unshed tears.

"If you're an only child, why would your mother not
want a relationship with you?" Even as he asked, it sounded
hypocritical. His own parents avoided him, and he was
their only living child.

"We had a bit of a falling-out when I refused to resign
from the ATF. I know she spoke from a broken heart. Losing my father was her biggest nightmare come true. She
begged me to quit, and when that didn't work, she resorted
to belittling my ambitions. She said I had to choose. The
ATF or family, meaning her."

"Sounds like she was reliving her ultimatum to your
father through you."

Randee tilted her head. "Never thought of it that way, but
yeah, I guess so. She contended I'd have divided loyalties—
eventually something would have to give."

"As in her perception of your father's career pushing
her aside?"

She nodded.

"How long ago did you have your falling-out?"

"Ten years."

Ace inhaled deeply. "Have you tried talking to her recently? I mean, surely enough time has passed that she'll
listen now." Was that true? No amount of time had healed
the brokenness in his family. He'd become a place for them
to park their anger. Contrary to the popular saying, time
didn't heal all wounds.

"I call once a month and every holiday. The conversation always revolves around her friends and their grand-
children and ends with some variation of 'stop being
self-absorbed and realize your biological clock is ticking.
You'll never find a husband.' to which I reply, 'I'm doing

great, Mom, thanks for asking.'" She rolled her eyes, but he sensed the hurt behind it.

That was more than his folks said to him. His mother would flip her estranged lid if he got married. "Do you want a family?"

Randee appeared taken off guard. "What?"

Ace hesitated, wondering if he'd pried too much. "You said your mom laid the guilt pretty thick with you about not being able to be a wife and agent. Did you even want that life?"

She shrugged. "Once upon a time when I actually thought having both was a possibility. But that dream vanished."

Why was he asking her any of this? He'd never marry. Didn't deserve happiness.

"I guess we can't have it all."

"Until you said it aloud, I never really thought I agreed with that statement." He sipped his coffee.

Her eyes met his with a strong intensity. "You do?"

"Not in the same context as you described, but I've spent my entire life focused on my career. A family has never been a consideration." He took another sip, preventing any further self-revelations.

"You mentioned you don't have much of a relationship with your folks, either." A statement, not a question.

"My mother blames me for Cara's death. Maybe she's right. She'd be alive if I had been with her that night." He rushed on before Randee offered any consolation. "My parents stay together because I'm the common enemy where they place their blame." His lack of communication skills had him spouting a series of horrible clichés.

"I don't get it." She sat back. "Why would heaving their hurt on you help them?"

"Their relationship suffered the brunt of their sorrow,

and they exist as two strangers in a platonic illusion of a marriage. Almost worse than if they'd parted ways. I'd rather be a bachelor the rest of my life than live like that."

"Wow."

"It's strange but it works. They claim to still be in love, at least on social media." He shrugged.

"I figure I'm pretty hard to like, let alone love."

"Have you ever been in love?"

She laughed. "Let's just say I've never had an offer of marriage."

"Then you've dated some really stupid men."

"I beg your pardon?"

"Sorry, an observation."

She grunted. "And what? If this whole dodging-death thing hadn't happened you'd be asking me out?"

"Oh, absolutely not." He shook his head vehemently.

She leaned back. "Yikes. Don't candy-coat the rejection."

Ace's ears warmed. *Smooth, Steele.* He stammered, "I mean, you deserve better. I'm the third-wheel guy. The one who hangs out with couples because he never has a date."

"If that's the case, it's totally voluntary."

Not exactly. "Some people don't deserve true love." Why was he saying this?

Randee leaned forward, and her voice softened. "Love isn't deserved. It's a gift. A choice. Everybody has regrets and mistakes. It's what makes us human and gives us connection. The best counselors are the ones who've overcome those problems. They've walked the hard road, and their experience equips them to empathize with others. And more than anything, God loves you, Ace. Nothing you could do or have done will ever change that. He couldn't love more today than He did yesterday or will tomorrow."

His throat thickened with emotion. "You really believe that?"

"With all my heart."

Suddenly very uncomfortable with the topic, he redirected the discussion. "Always figured Cara would marry young and have a bunch of kids. I pictured a whole herd of them calling me Uncle Ace."

"You two were close?"

He rarely spoke of Cara. It didn't seem right. She was gone. "For the short amount of time we had together. She was only eighteen when she died." His throat constricted, and he couldn't go on. Didn't want to.

Gratefully, Randee seemed to take the hint. "You're married to your career, too."

"I guess so? Except I'm no one special like you. Just a scientist. But I want to make a difference for the better."

She reached over and squeezed his shoulder. "You're an amazing guy, and you are making a difference."

He shrugged. "When the ATF came to PrimeRight with the idea for Ghost, it was the chance of a lifetime." Anxious to shift the spotlight away from him, he asked, "What about you?"

Randee paused, removed her hand and sipped her coffee. "I want to make bureau chief."

"I'm not sure what all that entails, but you're ambitious and smart. Definitely capable. That's an achievable ambition."

She smiled. "Thank you for saying so. It seems pretty impossible at this point."

"Nothing's impossible. You're the most amazing woman I've ever met." He did not just say that aloud.

Based upon the red creeping in on Randee's cheeks, he had.

"For what it's worth, Ace, I'm sorry you and your sister didn't get more time together." The genuine sympathy in her voice told him she understood.

"She would've loved you." He reached over and blanketed her hand with his. To his relief, she didn't move away. Instead, her blue eyes drank him in, and his heart swelled with an emotion he couldn't name. They held the position for several long seconds.

His hand moved to her cheek, and he ran his finger along the soft curve of her face. Randee's mouth parted slightly.

Ace leaned in closer, longing to kiss her. A breath away, he focused on the fullness of her lips.

"Miranda!"

Randee and Ace jerked back at Elias's intrusion.

"In my office. Now."

"Of course, Elias." She shoved away from the table and nearly ran from the room, leaving Ace with a confused heart and cold hands.

Vasili sauntered in and jumped onto his lap. Ace rubbed the cat's fur, cringing at Elias's booming voice bellowing throughout the house. "Have you lost your mind, cavorting with a possible criminal?"

The outburst confirmed the man's opinion of Ace.

He stood and set Vasili gently on the tile. Eager to put distance between his ears and Elias's vocal disapproval, he chose the quickest departure route, the stairs across from the kitchen. In a quiet but swift descent, he scurried down the carpeted steps into the fully finished walkout basement.

An expansive navy sectional sofa separated the area, and the intricately carved pool table centered the opposite side. Crisp lines revealed a recent vacuuming.

Vasili kept pace with him as if providing a tour of the house. He located two bedrooms and a bathroom, finally ending in the family room, where light beamed through the farmhouse-style door.

With everything in him, he fought the urge to throw it open and run.

THIRTEEN

Lack of sleep and the early-morning melee with Elias left Randee's energy waning. The warm sunlight beaming through the windshield added to her exhaustion. True to Nebraska's unpredictable seasons, the afternoon temperature had melted the evidence of the prior day's snowstorm.

She worked the steering wheel, anticipation intensifying at the next assignation with Ishi. Their conversation had been short, with Elias standing guard over Randee. Ishi demanded a face-to-face meeting for the purpose of transferring Ghost. She'd specified Randee come alone, but Ace hadn't given her an opportunity to leave him behind, thanks to the less-than-cordial hospitality Elias extended. In order to prevent anyone from tracing their call, they'd ended with a location and time.

Elias was convinced Randee needed to turn in Ace, and no matter what she said, he stubbornly refused to hear her out.

Maybe by talking to Ishi in person, Randee would gain her support in protecting Ace and delaying turning him in. At least until they had the evidence on Malte's spy. If nothing else, perhaps Ishi had forgotten that without Ace they couldn't access anything inside the briefcase?

"If I hadn't witnessed it myself, I wouldn't believe we

had a blizzard twenty-four hours ago," Ace said, interrupting her internal monologue.

Randee grinned. "Don't like the weather? Wait a minute. It'll change."

The common saying among locals had Ace chuckling.

Following Ishi's directions, Randee drove around the back side of the nondescript barn. "Guess this is where farm equipment comes to die," she murmured. Rusted tractors, sprayers, tillers and booms were spread out across the vast acreage in various degrees of decay.

She hesitated. If she continued, they might be trapped. After Malte's ambush the night before, she couldn't shake the suspicious thoughts. She slowed to a stop, then lifted her foot off the brake, allowing the SUV to creep forward.

"What's wrong?" Ace asked.

"Keep your eyes out for anyone approaching from behind." She inched beside an enormous piece of dark yellow apparatus. Its single-centered front tire stood taller than the SUV, and it was nearly the length of a semi.

"Watch out for the TerraGator."

"Is that what you call that beast?" Randee narrowly maneuvered past the blind spot created by the equipment's huge rear floater tires.

Relief at the sight of Ishi's classic Volkswagen Beetle camouflaged in the yard allowed Randee to exhale the breath she hadn't realized she'd been holding.

Ishi smiled and waved as Randee parked beside her. Her coworker's demeanor changed instantly—undoubtedly the moment she saw Ace in the passenger seat. Her disdain was as evident as an LED billboard. Ishi mouthed, "nice," and gave a slight shake of her head, emphasizing her objection.

Here we go again. Randee shut off the engine and prepared to defend Ace to another of her cohorts.

"*That's* Ishi?"

She grinned at the surprised inflection in Ace's tone.

Ishi's unconventional ways were normal within the team, so Randee rarely thought twice about the woman's eclectic fashion.

Ishi walked to the front of the SUV, impatience written in her aqua-colored lips, contrasting the sparkle of her rhinestone nose piercing. Her latest hairdo was a combination of half her head shaved bald, the rest shoulder-length and dyed electric blue with ice-blond highlights. Ironically, the tech's quiet disposition contradicted her wild taste, something she'd maintained since her black-hat computer hacking days.

"She's as amazing at her job as she is in person." Randee reached for the door handle. "Hand me the briefcase."

Ace slid the case away from her. "What? You never said anything about giving her Ghost."

"It's not like she can open it without you. Doesn't it make sense to pass the prototype to the ATF? Maybe it would remove the target on our backs."

"If that's true, why aren't we meeting at your office?"

"We're wanted, remember? She's risking her job just being here today. It's best for us to hand over Ghost."

"No. Until we're certain who to trust, I'm not giving the prototype to anyone."

Randee bit her lip, mentally agreeing with him. "Okay, we'll do it your way, but I'll have to talk with her alone."

"If there's evidence that can help me, I need to be a part of this conversation." Ace grabbed the briefcase handle.

Randee swiveled to face him, Ishi's annoyed pose—complete with arms crossed over her chest and tapping foot—in her peripheral vision. "Not yet. She's already mad at me for bringing you along. When I refuse to hand over Ghost, it'll only make things worse. Besides, you need to be our lookout."

He frowned but must've sensed the tension and remained silent.

Randee massaged her temple as her headache shifted

like a bowling ball determined to burst through her skull. "I'm not convinced Malte won't find us. If you see or hear anything suspicious, come into the barn immediately. I'll make this quick."

"Fine," he mumbled.

"Thank you." Randee slipped out of the SUV and rounded the hood.

Without a word of greeting, Ishi led the way into the barn. Dust and the muggy aroma of old hay swarmed Randee's senses and sent her into a sneezing bout.

"Bless you." Ishi propped her laptop on a bale at the rear of the building where a small window faced the road.

"Thank you."

Ishi turned and narrowed her eyes.

"Before you say anything—"

"Have you lost your mind?" she squeaked, swatting Randee on the arm. "Elias told me he caught you and Steele kissing." She hissed the last word as if speaking it aloud would trigger men in black to appear from the dark corners of the barn.

"Oh, he did not." Which was more than a little disappointing, but she wouldn't dare confess that to Ishi. "Elias interrupted before anything happened."

"So you admit there was something to interrupt?" A blue section of Ishi's hair swayed over her shoulder.

Randee cringed. Walked right into that one.

"And what part of 'come alone and bring the briefcase' didn't you understand?" Ishi busied herself booting up the computer.

"I didn't have a choice."

Ishi paused and met Randee's eyes. "Did Ace threaten you?"

"Of course not."

"Elias doesn't approve of him." The woman's keen perception once again confirmed that her skills exceeded technology.

"He's just cautious."

"And intimidating with a gazillion years of experience," Ishi finished.

"Something like that. I asked Ace to keep watch, anyway." Randee leaned against the wooden wall and crossed her ankles, hoping to look relaxed.

"Miranda, what are you doing? Ace Steele is our primary suspect. Have you forgotten that? You'll lose your badge for abetting a criminal."

Randee moved her hand over the pocket where the borrowed Ruger weighed down her hoodie. "There's no specific proof Ace has done anything illegal. And for the record, I don't think he's guilty."

"You're blinded by your feelings for him. Take Ghost out of the equation and see how Ace reacts." Ishi paced a path on the hay-covered floor, kicking up more dust.

Randee sneezed again. She couldn't dispute Ishi's words with facts, and she agreed with Ace's hesitation to pass Ghost along to anyone else. "It's his burden to bear and mine to protect him."

"The ATF owns the project."

"And when we can safely deliver it, we will. But if Malte compromised your secure line, isn't it possible he'd get his hands on the prototype?"

Ishi didn't appear convinced.

The tenderness Ace had shown in their quiet conversation this morning wasn't the act of a manipulative criminal. He'd shared the sorrow of his sister's death and told her about his ambitions. A guilty man wouldn't waste time doing that.

Would he?

All she had was her gut, which wasn't a comfort since

Elias had debunked her belief in following her instincts with his deceitful heart theory.

"Did Elias also tell you Ace offered to turn himself in? If he's conspiring with Malte, why would he do that?" Randee's blurted defense sounded more pathetic than convincing.

Ishi stopped and rolled her eyes. "Um, hello? Manipulation 101. Look, I realize you're stressed about Sergio and Wesley, but we have to keep working this case until we're pulled off or told otherwise."

"I agree. Allow me to gather evidence. Remember, we're on the blind side of justice." Nothing short of cold hard proof would sway Ishi or prevent Ace from going to prison. "I'm not naive. If he's guilty, I'll turn Ace in myself. But I think he's being framed."

Ishi sighed. "You might have a different mind-set once you see this."

Randee's stomach tanked. What had Ishi found? Her gaze immediately shifted to the door, and her hand rested on the gun.

"Wait. I'm sorry." Ishi combed her fingers through her hair. "This isn't how I expected this meeting to go. First, let's start over. Are you okay?"

This was the woman Randee loved. Kind. Compassionate and thoughtful. Her throat tightened at the comfort of a familiar friend. The stresses of the past two days welled up. "Relatively speaking. I've never been in a situation where there's no safe place. Or where I don't have backup."

Ishi embraced her, the scent of berries and cream from her shampoo wafting through the air. "Malte's ambush burst my security illusion bubble, too. I haven't figured out how he hacked into your text messages."

"Yeah, nothing is sacred."

"I hope that isn't true, because if this place is compromised, we're both dead or headed to a booking cell."

If the ATF discovered Ishi was talking to her, she'd be implicated as well.

"Thank you for coming." Randee's tension headache gained new momentum.

Ishi displayed a graph on her computer screen. "You wanted evidence of Ace's involvement. The last calls originated from his office phone."

"That only proves someone used his phone. Could've been Fritz Nelson."

Ishi's fingers flew across the keys as she queued a video. "That may be true, but he can neither confirm nor deny anything since he's down for the count."

The screen showed Fritz unconscious in a hospital bed surrounded by machines and wires. Yolanda sat beside him.

"He's had no visitors, and only approved personnel have been in his room. All have been vetted. There's an officer posted outside the door as well. If Malte was involved, wouldn't he finish off the partner?" Ishi opened several more video files, each similar and noneventful, with Yolanda at Fritz's side while the doctors and nurses performed their tasks.

"What is she saying?" Randee asked, leaning closer to the screen.

Ishi turned up the volume.

Yolanda's soft voice filtered through the computer's speakers. "Lord, we need you. Please do the impossible. Help us. Rescue and heal us."

"She's praying," Randee whispered, her heart squeezing at the tender supplication.

"The only time she leaves his side is to visit her son on the third floor."

Yolanda's distraught appearance testified to her endless vigil.

Ishi closed the computer. "Randee, you have to turn in Steele. You're risking your career for a man you barely know."

Was she right? Was Ace playing her? Using her to get away with Ghost? Her gaze flew to the doors. And she'd left him alone with the vehicle and the prototype.

"Please, consider everything objectively. If he is innocent, the truth will come out. Let me take Ghost back to the office. It'll be safe there."

Reservations locked Randee's legs in place. Ishi was her friend. Yet with a niggling in her mind, she couldn't help but wonder if Ishi wasn't trustworthy. Guilt and distrust combined as Randee considered the earlier ambush. And her mind screamed *no* at the thought of handing over the prototype.

"We may have lost Wesley and Sergio. I can't lose you, too."

Randee's mouth went dry, and worry raced through her mind. "I don't want to put you in any danger. Possession of Ghost puts an invisible missile target on your forehead."

Ishi quirked a pierced eyebrow. "Is there anything I can say to convince you?"

"I promise I'm being careful."

With a disapproving sigh, Ishi closed her laptop. "Take care of you."

"Take care of you," Randee repeated, then gasped. "When I got the text, it ended with 'take care of you.' How would they know our sign-off code?"

Ishi's eyes widened, but pounding footsteps and a man's voice halted their conversation.

Randee withdrew the gun, and Ishi moved to the side, pulling her Glock out of her hip holster.

Sunlight burst through the darkened barn door, and Randee prepared to fire.

She exhaled relief, fear replacing the reprieve at the sight of Ace's entrance. "Is someone here?"

He blocked the doorway. His deflated position and

grave expression wavered somewhere between angry and somber. "I need to talk with you, Randee. Alone."

"I'll give you a minute and keep watch." Ishi snatched her laptop and made a hasty exit.

"It couldn't wait? We're just about done, and Ishi needs to get out of here." Irritation replaced her fear, and Randee slid the Ruger back into her pocket.

"What did your friend say?"

"Nothing that will help you. Let's go."

Ace stepped closer. "Your coworker and Elias are right. You're foolish to believe in me. For your own good, turning me in is the best option." His tone hardened.

Was he challenging her? A tiny flicker of doubt sprang to mind, and for the first time Randee wondered if he'd hurt her and run. No. She shoved it down. "Whatever you heard—"

"Enough to know there's evidence implicating me. Helping me is dangerous and reckless, and it'll end badly for you." He gripped the briefcase, shoulders back, jaw taut.

She studied his face. "Ace, you're no criminal." Her voice shook slightly. Did he notice?

"Are you sure?"

Randee took a step forward, confidence building. "I trust my heart and my instincts."

"The heart is deceitful above all things."

Had he overheard Elias this morning, too? She halted, watching his body language. "My instincts are generally correct."

"That's reassuring," he laughed bitterly. "You don't know anything about me. Why would you sacrifice your dreams and career for a nobody like me?" Something akin to pain skittered in his blue irises.

Randee digested the question and replied honestly, "Because I believe in you."

His Adam's apple bobbed, and he averted his eyes. "You shouldn't."

Ishi burst through the door. "We have to get out of here. There's a pickup headed this way."

The trio rushed out of the barn, and Ishi paused at her Beetle. "Take the back exit. The fence is torn down there. I'll go through the front. They can't chase us both."

Randee moved to the SUV. "Ace, you drive, so I can shoot, if needed."

He slid behind the wheel as she jumped into the passenger seat. He fired up the engine and raced across the property.

The pickup in the background made a fast turn, approaching at excessive speed.

Ace rounded a second Morton building, and the vehicle swerved on the muddy ground.

"Watch out for the spray booms!" Randee pointed at the retractable metal arms connected to the enormous Terra-Gator peeking around the corner.

He jerked the wheel, narrowly missing the equipment, then accelerated toward the break in the fence.

The truck roared behind them. The crunching of metal confirmed they'd hit the same soggy patch, but the driver nicked the spray booms, then pursued, undeterred.

"Get down!" Randee ordered.

"I can't drive like that."

A bullet shattered the back window.

Ace ducked, and Randee swiveled around, returning fire. Her bullet pierced the truck's windshield, and the driver wove out of control before slamming into a large combine.

"Go!" Randee slid upward in her seat.

A man exited the passenger side and aimed again, but the bullets never reached the SUV.

They bounced across the field to a dirt road, neither speaking until Ace turned onto a county highway.

"How do they keep finding us?"

Randee's heart drummed in her ears, overtaking the headache. "Good question."

Had Malte traced them?

"I know what you're thinking."

She pinched the bridge of her nose. "I doubt that."

"You're wondering if I led them to the barn."

"Did you?"

"Of course not." Ace sighed. "I'm willing to take the fall, and if you find evidence to free me, you will."

"Maybe getting rid of Ghost would be best," Randee mumbled.

"Isn't it strange that Elias and Ishi both want possession? Until we're certain, please promise me you won't pass Ghost to anyone else." The urgency in his tone spoke of a deeper concern, and although she couldn't say why she agreed with his assessment, she did.

"Okay. I promise." She reached for his arm. "Let's get out of here."

The long acres of fields colored in remnants of the harvested corn and muddied ground surrounded them on both sides. After several minutes, Randee got comfortable in her seat and set her gun on her lap.

"Ace, since you probably overheard Ishi's comments—" she hurried on, afraid she'd lose the courage to speak "—let me clarify that my personal feelings are not skewing my objectivity."

"What kind of feelings do you have?"

Randee's ears burned. "Ones that are untimely and unprofessional. But it is what it is."

He chuckled.

Humiliation coursed through her, and she longed to hide under the seat. "Are you laughing at me?"

"No. Sorry. I just hate irony."

"I'm confused." *And I feel stupid.*

"Randee, you'd be foolish to fall on your sword for a guy like me."

She studied him, wondering if she'd heard him right. "What's that mean?"

"Nothing."

"Let's head back to Elias's and regroup. Hopefully he's come up with something else to help us."

They remained silent until Ace parked in Elias's garage. The tension in Randee's shoulders lessened as they entered the mudroom. "Elias?"

An eerie silence greeted them.

The tiny hairs on Randee's neck rose, her cop sense on high alert. Hefting her gun, she motioned for Ace to get behind her. "Something's wrong. Wait here."

"No way. I'm going in with you."

Without acknowledging him, she continued into the kitchen, pausing to digest the horrible destruction. Drawers had been dumped and the cupboards hung wide with the simple contents removed. Her shoes crunched on shattered glass, and porcelain dishes littered the tile floor. The sliding door stood open, adding to the chilled air.

She cleared the area, then entered the living room, taking slow, precise steps. Tunnel vision narrowed her line of sight as she absorbed the disarray and the stark reality that her safe place had been jeopardized.

Randee gripped the gun, heart thundering so hard against her rib cage she thought it would explode. Rounding the corner, she froze.

Elias lay facedown in a pool of blood, a gaping wound to the back of his head.

FOURTEEN

Ace pulled Randee into his arms with a fierce protectiveness he'd never experienced, and it nearly consumed him.

"Let go." She struggled against him. "I need to see if Elias is alive."

He held tight, battling a sense of helplessness to sweep her from the scene. "He's gone."

"No. You don't know that." She looked up, and a tear trailed down her cheek.

"No one survives that much blood loss." An unwanted flashback of Cara's murder scene invaded his mind. He shoved the memory away. "We need to get out of here." *I need to get out of here.* "Whoever did this might return. Please, Randee." Ace pulled her back, refusing to let her near the body, and surveyed the room.

His perusal halted on a manila envelope with his name scrawled across it, taped to the opposite wall. He sidestepped, target-locked on it, and dragged her along.

Randee stopped fighting, as if a switch had been flipped in her brain. "Don't touch anything," she said, returning to her cop persona.

Ace ignored her and ripped open the envelope, retrieving a cell phone and a five-by-seven picture.

Randee snatched it away, and her hand went to her

throat. Ace leaned over, inspecting the photograph of two men, bound and gagged.

"Sergio and Wesley," she whispered.

"Your team?" Ace studied the phone and pressed the on button. A single text message appeared with a number. He passed the device to Randee, then jerked to look at the stairs. "Ghost."

Ace hefted the briefcase, pulse raging, and bolted to the second floor, taking two and three steps at a time.

Randee's footfalls echoed behind him. She called out, but he didn't stop.

Ace leaped over the debris cascading into the hallway from each bedroom's doorway. He skidded to a halt in the bathroom, inadvertently kicking a medicine bottle. The pills rattled like a maraca before crashing into the base of the toilet.

Scattered contents from the linen cabinet covered the floor, yet nothing indicated Ghost had been disturbed. But he had to know for sure.

Randee touched his arm, startling him. "Ace, what's going on?"

He glanced over his shoulder, incapable of forming words past the desert in his mouth and unable to resist the urge. Curiosity propelled him forward. Had the killer found Ghost?

Ace entered in a reverent walk of doom. He set down the briefcase, then reached for the cool porcelain lid and flipped it over, sucking in a breath.

Ghost remained sealed underneath. He heaved a sigh of relief and replaced the lid. "We have to go." He snagged the briefcase and moved past her.

"But the—"

Ace shook his head. Malte must assume Ace still had possession of Ghost. He didn't dare relocate the prototype.

They exited the house and climbed back into the SUV.

Randee gripped the steering wheel. "What was that all about? Why did you hide Ghost in the toilet? Shouldn't we take it with us?"

"They missed it in their initial search. We need to leave everything as is. Malte believes the prototype's in the empty briefcase. Delaying is the only tool we have to bargain for your team's release."

Randee's eyebrows peaked. "I don't like it, but I can't offer a better solution, either."

"Don't want to keep Malte waiting." Ace lifted the phone, dialed and hit Speaker.

Two rings.

"Mr. Steele, so good to hear from you." The man's too-calm demeanor oozed through the line. "You are quite challenging."

Anger sprouted confidence in Ace. "Let's finish this. On my terms. First, if you think you can take Ghost and go, you're wrong. The briefcase has safety measures in place and without me alive, you cannot access the lock."

The man snorted. "We'll see about that. All I need is your fingerprint, and you don't have to be alive for me to obtain that. You're wasting my time."

"Trust me, you want to hear what I have to say."

Malte exhaled his obvious impatience. "Or I kill you and just take what I want."

"Yeah? How's that working out for you?"

The man's breathing grew louder.

Ace had struck a nerve. "As I was saying, if you fail to enter the correct code more than three times, the lock disengages permanently and the case disintegrates the contents. The outer shell is also bulletproof and fire-resistant. So it seems my terms are the only terms. Let's start with my first condition. Release the hostages, and I'll make the trade."

Malte's sardonic laugh echoed. "Aren't you the crafty negotiator? Watched a lot of crime drama shows? Let's pretend I care about your 'terms.' Which I don't. Be at Prime-Right within twenty minutes. Two lives depend on you. Bring your girlfriend, and make no mistake, Mr. Steele, if you notify the authorities, I will kill as many people as it takes to get Ghost. I'll be watching you."

Ace looked at Randee. "And how will you do that?"

"Just drive." The line disconnected.

He gripped the phone, shoulders tightening. "It's a trap."

Randee started the engine and headed toward the road. "What choice do we have? I have to help Sergio and Wesley. I'm not leaving them, or you, to handle this. I abandoned them once. I won't do it again."

"All he wants is Ghost. I can deliver the prototype and if it goes bad, you'll still have a chance to take them down."

Randee shook her head and accelerated. "This isn't negotiable."

Ace leaned back and exhaled, staring at the roof of the SUV. The woman was exhausting.

"I will not sit around while these men get away with killing—" Her lip trembled.

Tenderness shattered his impatience, and he gripped her hand. "Arrest Malte. That cannot happen if you're with me. Please, let me do this. You have no problem risking your life for mine. Why is it wrong for me to do the same?" His heart tightened at the thought of Randee being hurt. He'd failed Cara. For the first time, he could do the right thing. Protect Randee. Just as Elias had said.

"This goes beyond you and me. Don't you understand? My team is in danger. I'm no coward. They need me."

She had no faith in his ability to handle the situation. Irritation blinded him, and he had to turn away, staring out the window. Randee drew the line and confirmed she didn't trust him to protect her. Regardless, somehow, when Malte took the empty briefcase, Ace would negotiate for her life.

"Once your team is safe, return for Ghost. I'll offer to take Malte there, and you can arrest him." Unless Malte killed him first. Regardless, Randee would be out of danger, her name would be cleared and she'd make bureau chief. That's all that mattered. Resolved, Ace replaced his heart armor and prepared to say goodbye when this was finished. "He said he's watching us. How's that possible?"

"My guess is he's got GPS capability on that phone."

Ace glanced down at the device. Of course. GPS gave Malte real-time location. "Why does he want to meet at PrimeRight?"

Randee shrugged. "He must think there's information hidden at the lab."

"That makes sense. He's ambushed us more than once there. Let him believe what he wants to if it postpones the inevitable."

"Once we get to him, we'll need proof of life for Wesley and Sergio."

Her team. Was that all she cared about? What about Ace? Malte would kill him once he got Ghost. He shook off the thought. No, he was doing this for Randee. "Don't worry. I'll promise to help Malte after he releases your team." His voice was hollow in his ears. "You'll have a limited amount of time to get to safety once they see the empty case."

"How do we stall them until then?"

"I'll have to do some fast talking and a lot of praying."

"Whatever happens, don't let him separate us. He'll use psychological ploys, playing us against each other."

"Could you clarify?"

"Threatening to hurt me if you don't open the case, stuff like that."

"Got it." He swallowed hard.

Their conversation halted and they made record time traveling to PrimeRight.

Upon entering the garage, the cell rang again. Ace answered.

"If you were stupid enough to bring any weapons, leave them and this phone in the vehicle." Malte disconnected.

Randee removed the gun, set it on the dashboard, then stuffed the keys between the console and the seat. "Don't want to make this too easy for him. Are you ready?"

Ace nodded, unable to force the lie past his lips. He wasn't ready to die.

He lifted the empty case and with a final prayer, joined Randee at the back of the SUV, then led the way into the building.

Their footsteps echoed on the tile floor as they entered PrimeRight. Battling the instinct to run, Ace stood taller, intending to face Malte without fear. Or at least fake it.

They paused in the lobby, where the late-afternoon light beamed through the windows, casting shadows on the men cradling their MP5s. The first, a colossal imbecile, towered over the younger, cocky one boasting a big grin.

"I recognize the kid," Ace said under his breath.

"The partner of your hijacker," Randee confirmed.

"Put down the briefcase," the youngest said beside his redwood-sized backup. His spiked red hair and overconfident strut resembled a rooster.

"No." Ace clutched the case to his chest. "I'm not giving this to anyone except Malte."

The larger man laughed and swiped at his unruly beard. "You got gumption. Take a lesson, Nile."

Nile scowled. "Move." He used the MP5 as a pointer, aiming at the hallway that led to the basement stairwell.

Dread clung to Ace. The lower level had no doors, which greatly reduced their chances of escape. They'd be cornered. Trapped. The realization had him hesitating. He turned, lowering the briefcase in one hand. "No."

"No?" the kid echoed.

The humor was erased from the larger man's face. "Do what you're told, scientist. Nile, take care of the girlfriend."

"Oh, yeah, I got plans for her." The boy gave a low whistle.

Ace shifted closer. "She stays with me."

"Malte gives the orders."

"It's okay, Ace, I just need a little room to breathe." Randee's tone held a menacing air.

He picked up on her cue. She'd overpower Nile, but the behemoth of a partner was a different tale. If Randee managed to snag the gun, they had a fighting chance.

Ace stepped back, hands lifted in mock surrender. "Whatever, I'm only trying to help." It'd require brains, not brawn, to overpower the brute.

Nile approached, sporting a nasty grin. Randee moved at lightning speed, delivering a roundhouse kick to the side of his head. He stumbled into the larger man, catching them both off guard.

The partner shoved Nile away. Ace charged forward and swung the briefcase, connecting with the Goliath of a man. The hollow *thud* sounded like a baseball bat on a melon. He fell at Ace's feet, sending his MP5 skidding across the floor.

Ace froze at the sound of gunfire above him, and white particles from the bullet-riddled ceiling showered him. Randee stood inches from the discarded gun.

"That was impressive, but try that again and the next

round has your name on it." A new duo flanked them, blocking the doors, and closed in. "Lady, move next to your boyfriend."

Randee complied, stepping beside Ace.

"They keep multiplying," he whispered.

"Yeah, like the cockroaches in my first apartment," Randee hissed.

"Four against two aren't favorable odds," he said.

The skinnier of the guards yanked his arms behind his back, ripping the briefcase from his hands. The snap of handcuffs echoed in the lobby. "Why we gotta keep them alive? I got the goods."

The man securing Randee's hands in front of her answered, "Because Malte said to bring them down."

"We'd hate to disappoint Malte." Ace injected a hint of sarcasm.

Nile joined the two guards, rubbing his face. They forced Randee and Ace through the hallway to the stairwell.

The steps were narrow, forcing them to walk single file.

"Lead the way," Ace's guard ordered.

Nile stormed past, giving them a full view of the developing bruise from Randee's kick. He shot her a murderous glare. Like a herd of cattle, they tromped down the stairs, echoing footsteps in the hollow area. Ace jerked at the door slam. A final sentence to their doomed destiny.

Again, Ace considered fighting back, but refrained. They had to free Randee's team.

The lower level was dark and dank, more ominous than he recalled. Not that he'd hung out there often. The men took them through the main section that housed the boiler and other equipment, then shoved Ace and Randee into the maintenance office at the far end of the floor.

The guards moved to strategic stations, covering all corners and preventing escape. Ace's gaze traveled to the man leaning back in one of the plastic chairs with his expensive black Bally dress shoes resting on the table centered in the room. Silver-streaked hair framed his face, cascading in waves to his shoulders. The neatly trimmed goatee emphasized his nasty smirk.

"Titus Malte?" Ace asked.

"Not how you pictured him, either?" Randee moved closer to his side.

"Thank you for joining me. Based upon the gunfire I heard, I assume the transition wasn't a smooth one?" Malte's dark eyes seemed to count the remaining guards, and a question hung in his expression.

Nile spoke up. "Scientist dude knocked out Griffin."

"I see." The debonair, articulate monster Ace had imagined didn't match with the man in the tailor-fitted suit in front of him. "Gentlemen, please leave us. I have much to discuss with Agent Jareau and Mr. Steele."

Nile and the skinnier guard stepped out of the room while the biggest of the men stayed and placed the briefcase on the table. He moved to cover the door.

Ace fidgeted.

"Don't even think about it. Byron will shoot you without question." Malte gestured to the chairs. "Please sit down. We're not barbarians standing around a campfire."

Randee leaned against the wall, defiance radiating from her.

The corner of Malte's lip curved as he reached for the briefcase, dragging it across the table. "Mr. Steele, it appears you were telling the truth about the lock. Please open it."

Ace shook his head. "Not until you've done what I've asked."

Malte snapped his fingers.

Like an obedient chimpanzee, Byron crossed the room and dragged Randee to a chair opposite Malte. He shoved her onto the seat and steadied his gun against her temple, eliciting her disdain-filled glare.

Ace stiffened. "Let her go. If you kill her, you'll get nothing from me."

"Byron, please." Malte waved at the guard. "We're all adults. Agent Jareau will be complacent for the good of the group."

Byron lowered the gun, still hovering behind Randee.

Malte addressed Ace. "Contrary to what I'm sure you've been told, I'm a fair man willing to treat you with respect. I expect the same courtesy."

Randee snorted. "Respect? Attacking us? Kidnapping my partner and boss? Killing my friend? You need a lesson on the definition of respect, Malte. Don't do anything until he releases my team, Ace."

As if he needed the reminder. "You heard her. Release the ATF agents." Ace hoped his voice held more assurance than he felt. He locked gazes with Randee.

A slight moment of confusion passed over Malte's face. He placed his hands flat on the table and leaned forward. "What are you two rambling about?"

Randee shifted in the chair. "Don't play stupid. That's why we're here. You left us the picture as a warning."

The blank look Malte returned conveyed his cluelessness. "If this is some tactic to gain your freedom, you're wasting your time. Mr. Steele, your gifts and talents are sorely misappropriated here. Whereas working for me, you're a warrior in my army, willing to fight for their rights as citizens of the great US of A."

Ace gaped. "You have to be kidding me."

"If you didn't kill my friend or kidnap my team, then

you have someone in your militia betraying you," Randee said, resuming control of the conversation.

Ace marveled at her quick rationale.

Malte's jaw tightened, and his eyes narrowed. He seemed to study the guard. "My men wouldn't dare double-cross me. The price is too great."

Byron understood the warning, based on the strained bob of his Adam's apple.

"There's a major disconnect. My team has been missing since the night of the PrimeRight gala. Where are they?" Randee pressed. "You left a picture for me."

Malte waved her off. "Stop trying to distract me."

Ace spoke up. "Who else is aware of the prototype? Anyone with the plans would have a plethora of weapons at their disposal. They'd surpass you and take over your group."

"In my experience, criminals have a short life span for devotion, and they're easily swayed by money and power. If we tell you where everything is, are you certain this man won't kill you once he gets the prototype?" Randee glanced up at Byron.

"Shut up," he answered.

"Ah, not a denial. Malte, you might want to reconsider our offer." Randee smiled, sweet and sassy.

Ace chastised himself. This wasn't the time for those thoughts.

Shaken, Malte jumped to his feet, his casual demeanor unraveling with each step he paced in the small room. "You're a liar!"

"Am I? You have great intel. If you didn't leave the picture, who did?" Randee challenged.

Malte produced a pistol from his suit pocket, aiming it at Byron. "You'd better be very clear here."

Byron stepped back. "Mr. Malte, you can trust me. I

can't speak for Griffin, Nile or Zeke. But me, you know." His vehemence was impressive, yet didn't seem to sway his boss.

"Who else would benefit from the prototype?" Randee asked, her voice soft. Teasing. "Got any rivals? Anyone you've messed with in the past who'd love to get back at you? Maybe someone you've cheated. Is there honor among thieves like you, Malte?"

Malte shook his head, tightening his hold on the pistol. "Bring in the others."

Byron nearly tripped over himself getting out of the room, returning within seconds with Nile and the skinnier guard.

"Where's Griffin?" Malte barked.

"He's still, um…out," Nile sputtered.

Malte fixed his gun on the men. "I'll ask this only once. The one who tells the truth gets to live. Which of you betrayed me?"

All three shook their heads with such vigor, Ace wondered if they'd topple off their necks.

"Someone's lying." Malte moved the pistol between them. "Speak and fast."

"Byron wasn't with us when we brought the prisoners," Nile stammered.

"I'm the only one Mr. Malte can depend on," Byron defended, his face turning a bright shade of red.

Malte fired, and Byron dropped to the ground. Dead. "Which of you will be next?"

Nile and Zeke lifted their hands in the air. "Mr. Malte, we've served you faithfully. Done everything you asked. It was Byron. We're faithful to the cause. Your law is the only law. We've proven our loyalty."

Malte appeared pleased by their cowering and lowered the gun. "Get rid of him and bring in our guest."

The men scurried out, dragging Byron from the room.

Randee didn't miss a beat. "They're great actors, but how can you be sure they're telling you the truth?" She was good at unnerving Malte. They'd gained an upper hand for the moment and thrown the criminal off his game. But she had to be thinking the same thing as Ace. Who else could be holding her team?

The door flew open.

In what felt like slow motion, Ace's gaze bounced between Randee and the entryway.

No.

It wasn't possible.

The person standing in front of him wasn't a mirage.

Malte wasn't the only one who'd been betrayed.

FIFTEEN

Randee's vision clouded. She clenched her hands, digging the cold steel of the handcuffs into her skin.

She'd prided herself on her ability to read people. Her life depended on the skills required to assess individuals and situations. Yet in an instant, all of her confidence slammed to the floor at the sight of the bedraggled woman with red-rimmed eyes and quivering lips.

Yolanda Ruiz stumbled through the doorway, the shorter of the two guards prodding her. Wild-eyed, her hands flew to her mouth when she spotted Ace and Randee. Her face went ashen, and sweat beaded on her forehead.

Nervousness?

Fear?

Shame?

She wasn't bound, which reflected either her as a willing partner to Malte or his assurance that she wouldn't run away.

Nile grabbed Yolanda's arm and shoved her down hard into the remaining chair.

"Thank you for joining us, Ms. Ruiz," Malte cooed, rising from his seat. He slithered behind Yolanda, grazing his hand across her shoulders and eliciting her visible cringe.

A small measure of relief covered Randee, and she un-clenched her hands. Yolanda wasn't a willing participant.

Malte laughed. "Now that we're all here, let's get down to business. Mr. Steele, you've made it abundantly clear you don't value your own life. But what about these women?" He moved closer to Randee.

"Don't touch her," Ace yelled.

"Ah, you do." Malte patted Randee's head like a dog. "And how about poor little Diego Ruiz?"

What she'd give to smack the twisted smile off Malte's face.

Ace's expression darkened and his shoulders rounded, defeated.

Anger returned, boiling in Randee's veins. "You're a cow-ard." He knew Ace wouldn't be able to withhold Ghost if it meant endangering innocent people, especially Yolanda's terminally ill son.

"Yolanda, what are you doing here?" Ace's incredulous stare conveyed his confusion at her role in this bizarre turn of events.

"She's the spy providing insider information to Malte about Ghost," Randee inserted.

Yolanda sat with shoulders hunched, eyes downcast.

"Yes, she performed very well," Malte commended, then spun to face Randee. "You were correct. There is a betrayer among us, but it wasn't one of my men." His lips twisted into a snarl, and he yanked Yolanda's hair back, evoking a yelp.

"Let her go!" Randee jumped up, but Nile shoved her down.

Malte leaned over, inches from Yolanda. "Have I under-estimated you, Mrs. Ruiz? Was your son not enough incen-tive? Are you playing me? Who else are you working for?"

"No. Of course not. I did everything you asked." The

intensity in Yolanda's tone reassured Randee she wasn't lying.

"Did you leave Agent Jareau a picture?" Malte demanded.

The slight jerk of her neck conveyed Yolanda's attempt to shake her head. Malte's death grip on her hair prevented movement. "No!"

He released his hold and stepped back, sporting a satisfied grin.

The woman met Randee's gaze. "I'm so sorry."

Confusion etched Ace's face. "Why, Yolanda? We trusted you."

"I had no choice," she pleaded, eyes welling with tears.

"Oh, the great scientist isn't as smart as we thought?" Malte laughed. "Please fill him in on your task, Mrs. Ruiz."

Yolanda gulped and averted her eyes. "I had to spy on you and report back to Mr. Malte about Ghost. He threatened Diego's life."

Ace flexed his jaw.

"Where is my team?" Randee asked, urgency building.

"I don't understand. What do you mean, Randee?" Yolanda's gaze bounced between the parties at the table.

If Malte didn't have Sergio and Wesley, who did? All Randee could do was plant seeds of doubt, but if they knew nothing, being here was wasting valuable time.

"Stop with the team nonsense! This is about what I want. It's all about me!" Malte addressed Randee. "Hmm, seems we have a bit of a quandary. Someone here is lying."

Yolanda rushed on. "Ace, give him Ghost. He'll kill Diego if you don't. Hate me. Kill me yourself. But please, for the sake of my baby, please give him what he wants."

Randee's chest tightened. How could she have misjudged Yolanda? Regret at demanding her own way struck her. She should've listened to Ace. Now she was a prisoner here with no way to help Wesley and Sergio.

Malte's tone, though controlled, was clearly agitated. "You heard her. The boy's life hangs in your defiant hands. Open the briefcase." The coldness in his voice guaranteed he wasn't bluffing.

Ace locked gazes with Randee. He had to comply, but once he revealed the empty briefcase, what would Malte do? She nodded.

"You'll discover the briefcase isn't what you want," Ace said.

"Oh, but it is." Malte walked behind Ace and inserted the handcuff key, releasing one hand. "Open it."

"I'll give you everything, after you release Randee and Yolanda, and prove they, along with Diego, are safe."

"*Randee*," he sneered, "isn't going anywhere. She's a liability and a nuisance. But I'm not unreasonable. I'd love nothing more than an ATF agent with insider knowledge in my pocket. Here's my counteroffer, and I'll give it once. Take it or die. Both of you will join me and I'll spare your miserable lives."

"You're an ATF agent?" Yolanda asked.

Randee shot her a "not now" look. "I'd rather die," she said through gritted teeth.

"My allegiance isn't up for purchase." Ace sat up straighter.

Malte shrugged. "Fine with me. Open the case."

"Please, Ace, do what he says," Yolanda wailed, oblivious of the fact that it was empty.

"I will give you whatever you want. Just let everyone else go." Ace remained calm. His voice unwavering.

"Open that case now!" Malte screeched, slamming his fists on the table.

"There's nothing inside," Randee blurted. What was she doing?

Ace jerked to look at her. "Randee."

"You're a liar," Malte choked, then shoved his gun against the back of Ace's head. "Open it!"

Ace entered the code and applied his fingerprint, releasing the lock.

With the exuberance of a child at Christmas, Malte lunged and flung it wide.

His face reddened so much Randee worried the man might explode. "Where. Is. The. Prototype?" he bellowed, shoving the briefcase off the table.

"I'll take you to where it's hidden. After you let Yolanda and Randee go," Ace urged.

Malte's shoulders shook. "So you can play more games? No, you stay here." He regained his composure, straightened his suit and stood taller, then yanked Yolanda to her feet. "Ms. Ruiz will accompany me, and if you try to escape, I'll kill Diego while his mother watches."

"Ace, don't—" Randee said.

Sorrow filled his blue eyes. "It's over." He faced Malte. "The prototype is in Elias Archer's home. Hidden in the upstairs bedroom."

Randee gasped. Desperation in Ace's expression conveyed understanding. He'd lied. But why? Once Malte searched the bedrooms, he'd kill Diego. What was he thinking? What purpose would deceiving the criminal serve? One last bargaining chip?

Ace must be stalling. But it was futile. Eventually he'd have to tell Malte the truth.

"If Ghost isn't there, I'll make the boy's death excruciating." Malte snapped the handcuffs back on Ace's wrists and dragged a hysterical Yolanda out of the room, the guards following. Before the door closed, he said, "I'll call when I have the prototype. Finish them."

As soon as the lock clicked, Randee asked, "What were you thinking? He'll kill Diego."

"Buying time. We have to escape and get to the police."

"With armed guards and both of us handcuffed?" Randee slumped in the chair and put her head down on the cold steel of the table. "Lord, help us. Please."

"I'm sorry. I didn't know what else to do," Ace said.

"This is hopeless. If Malte doesn't have Sergio and Wesley, who does?" She'd failed everyone. "I focused on myself and the promotion. I've failed my team, Diego's in danger, Yolanda is a pawn to Malte and we're dead. Somehow bureau chief has lost its luster. I don't deserve the opportunity to lead, anyway. My mother's right. I'm too selfish."

"The very nature of your job goes against that belief." Ace glanced away. "Fritz says, 'Your life will follow your most predominant thoughts.'"

Randee sighed. "My thoughts have been so erratic I struggle to keep up. First, I assumed this assignment would be easy. Catch Malte. Close case. Get promoted. Then I met you and suddenly I'm praying more for your happiness and protection. Not just in a job sense. Never thought I'd be like that. Guess that's what Elias meant about me losing objectivity."

"Welcome to my natural propensity to ruin people's lives." Ace's words would've sounded pitiful, except Randee saw conviction. He truly believed he was responsible for the mess of a case.

"None of this is your fault." Randee regarded him.

He slumped in the chair and leaned his head back. "How could Yolanda betray us like that?"

The answer came too easy for Randee. "Motherly instincts. Her love for Diego exceeds everything. Whatever happens, forgive her. She's only protecting her child."

"I guess that's understandable." His voice softened, and he drilled her with his blue eyes. "I wanted to do the same for you. You're not the only one with misplaced or ill-timed feelings, Randee. I—"

She pushed up from the chair. "Don't do that."

"What?"

"Start talking like this is the end. Doing that foxhole-confession thing." She leaned against the wall and stared at the ceiling. "Okay, Lord, I give. I tried it my way, and time's running out. Help—"

"I have an idea," Ace interrupted. "Malte killed Byron. Griffin is hopefully still unconscious, which leaves two guards. He would've taken one with him. You and I can overpower the remaining guard."

Hope returned. "I'm game. What're you thinking?"

"We need whoever is left to come in. I'll hold him off. You get out of here and call the police."

Randee shook her head. "I'm not going anywhere without you. We're doing this together. You owe me."

He quirked a brow. "How do you figure?"

"Life-and-death situations bring out strange emotions. Let's see how you feel after the bullets stop flying and people aren't trying to kill us. Call it an experiment to measure our actual chemistry."

He grinned. "Challenge accepted. Now, how do we subdue the guard while we're both handcuffed?"

"We'd need to get his gun."

The clicking door lock had them both freezing. Ace moved protectively in front of Randee and whispered, "Keep him occupied."

Nile entered before she had time to ask why. "What're you guys talking about?"

The kid was no match for them. But had he overheard their conversation? "Nile, you're a smart guy." Not really. "Malte will kill you, too. Remember what he did to Byron."

"Nah, when I finish you two off, he's gonna see how valuable I am." He stood taller and puffed out the illusion of a chest.

"You're nothing to Malte. No one is. The man threatened to kill a little boy," Randee pleaded.

"Shut up. You don't know anything."

"Malte will eliminate any witness to his crimes." Randee forced calm and gentleness to her tone. "Hadn't Byron been faithful to the cause, too?"

A minute expression of regret passed over Nile's young face. In her peripheral vision, Randee caught sight of Ace's hand and tried not to cringe. He'd dislocated his thumb and pulled his hand through the cuff, freeing himself.

She had to keep Nile busy. "Set us free, and I'll make sure the judge knows how brave you were and how you helped us. He'll give you leniency." If they didn't get out of here before Malte found Ghost, they were dead.

"Whatever—" Nile's laugh was cut short by Ace's one-stride tackle and the punch to the guy's stomach.

Nile retaliated by driving the butt of his gun down on Ace's head, causing him to stumble back.

Randee bolted upright and kicked Nile square in the chest, thrusting him into the wall. Ace swept Nile's legs out from under him, and he tumbled to the ground.

"Get his gun!" Randee yelled.

Ace grabbed the weapon and stalked Nile, kneeling on his hands and knees. "Please don't kill me."

"Unlike your boss, I wouldn't do that."

Randee moved toward him. "It's best if you close your eyes."

Nile blinked several times, then lip trembling, he obeyed.

Ace flat-palmed Nile's carotid artery, knocking him out.

"Does he have the handcuff key?" Randee dropped beside the unconscious guard.

Ace dug through his pockets and came up empty. "Nothing. Not even a phone."

Randee sat back on her heels. "Malte intended to kill all of us after he found Ghost." She glanced once more at Nile, a surge of sympathy for the disillusioned young man.

Ace helped her up. "Let's get out of here."

They rushed out the door, and Ace locked the unconscious Nile inside.

Ace's thumb throbbed from where he'd dislocated the digit to pull his hand free from the cuffs. They darted to the vehicle, grateful it still sat parked in the garage.

"What about keys?" he asked.

"I stuffed them between the seat and the console, remember?"

Ace dug beside the cushion, locating the keys. "Malte must've been in too much of a hurry to look for them." He helped her into the SUV and commenced breaking every speed law on the way to Elias's home. "If we get the attention of a police officer, we'll have him uncuff you and follow us."

"Works for me."

"What's your plan?" Ace worked the steering wheel.

"Malte only has Zeke left with him."

"We can take on one guard."

"Well, you can," Randee said. "I'm not much use to you handcuffed."

"I don't know, you've got some mean kicking skills."

She laughed and lifted her hands. "At least he was dumb enough to put my hands in front of me."

They neared Elias's property. Ace killed the lights and parked. They ran the remaining distance, then crept to the living room window.

Zeke stood at the foot of the stairs, playing on his cell phone, oblivious to them.

"This way. The house has a walkout basement," Randee whispered.

They bolted around to the farmhouse-style door, and Ace used his elbow to break one of the six window panels. Once inside, he asked, "How do we walk upstairs without attracting Zeke?"

"Move slowly. Stay to the edge of the steps where the structure is stronger and won't creak."

Ace snatched two pool balls and pocketed them before climbing the stairs.

If Zeke had stayed put, he'd be near the front door, leaving the entrance to the basement in his line of sight. They'd have to distract him.

An open banister provided no cover, and getting Zeke out of the way was imperative if they hoped to take Malte by surprise. And they'd have one shot to do it.

"I'll go first," Ace said, leading Randee up the stairs.

Handcuffed, she wouldn't be able to fight off Zeke.

He neared the top and peeked through the banister railing.

Zeke stood peering out the living room window with his back to them.

Ace surveyed the area that required crossing the open five-foot space in order to reach the kitchen. He sucked in a breath and tiptoed. Then, heart pounding, he sprinted into the kitchen.

Several seconds passed.

Where was Randee? Anxious, he risked peeking out just as she scurried beside him. He nearly bellowed his surprise.

"Sorry," she mouthed.

Ace withdrew one of the pool balls from his pocket and again, glanced around the corner. Zeke leaned against the front door about ten feet away facing the entrance to the kitchen, occupied again with his cell phone.

Ace tossed the ball, smacking the wall beside the stairs, and it bounced down with several muffled thuds.

The action worked, enticing Zeke to investigate. When he came within striking distance, Ace tackled him from behind. They landed with an *oomph* on the hardwood floors. A final strike to Zeke's neck stilled him.

"Well done," Randee whispered. "Does he have a key?"

Ace quickly searched Zeke's pockets, then shook his head. They moved toward the stairwell, and a commotion above disguised their approach.

"Where is it?" Malte hollered, and the crash of items hit the floor.

"I... I don't know," Yolanda sputtered.

Their voices carried from Elias's bedroom.

Ace inched along the hallway and squatted beside the door. Randee stayed right behind him.

"Tell me where it is!" Malte screeched.

Ace peered into the room. Malte stood with his back to Ace, Yolanda facing him. To her credit she did nothing to alert Malte when she spotted Ace.

Malte continued ranting and throwing things in his search. He moved to the closet and flung open the door.

Randee pushed past Ace. What was she thinking? He started to object, but she darted to his right and emitted an ear-splitting scream.

Malte spun around, eyes wide. Startled.

Ace wasted no time. He throat-punched Malte, stunning him.

Yolanda jumped into action and snatched the porcelain lamp from the nightstand. In a swift motion, she slammed it down on Malte's head.

He slumped to the floor.

"Good work," Ace commended. "See if he's got handcuff keys."

Yolanda searched Malte's pockets and produced the keys. She released Randee, who then transferred the cuffs to Malte. "Call 911."

Without a word, Yolanda scurried from the room, and her descending footsteps echoed.

Malte groaned from where he lay facedown, arms behind his back.

A woman's scream below got their attention.

Ace passed Randee the gun. They both moved toward the door, listening.

A baritone voice spoke, then Yolanda responded. Both were muffled.

Someone ascended the stairs and drew closer.

Ace glanced at Randee, and they flanked the entry. She held the weapon at the ready.

The battle wasn't over.

SIXTEEN

"Put down your gun, Miranda. It's just me."

Randee gasped at Elias's familiar baritone voice. He entered the bedroom, and her arms went slack while her grip tightened on the gun. "It's not possible. You're—"

"—dead?" Elias laughed.

She shook her head and blinked several times, struggling to clear her mind against the light-headedness weakening her knees. "I saw you. The gunshot. The blood. I checked your pulse!"

Elias leaned against the door frame, wearing a smug grin. "Actually, you didn't. Which was good for me. And everything else was faked."

Her thoughts were scrambled. Ace had told her no one could survive that kind of blood loss. She jerked to look at him, anger swirling with confusion. Was he involved?

No. His ashen face spoke his obvious surprise.

She studied Elias. Was he working with Malte? Had he used her to get to Ghost? But why fake his death? "What kind of twisted game is this?"

"One you played very well," Elias said.

An invisible binding constricted her chest more with each breath. Elias was involved. Yet he hadn't found Ghost. Had he?

"Randee trusted you. More than anyone. Including me."

She caught the hurt in Ace's voice. If only he knew. The only person she didn't trust was herself, because Ace Steele had exceeded being just an assignment.

"Based upon her expression, I'm not so sure I'd agree with you. You've got a murderous look in your eyes, Miranda."

She took a step, anger propelling her forward, curiosity overriding her fear. She lifted the gun. "What did you do, Elias? Tell me what's going on."

"Put down the gun, Miranda. You're not going to shoot me."

"Don't be so sure."

Elias didn't flinch. "Steele, go and retrieve Ghost. Kudos, by the way, in your choice of hiding place. I did locate the prototype in the toilet and quite honestly, was surprised you didn't move it when you all found me 'dead.'" He used air quotes.

Ace blinked. "If you knew where to find Ghost, why didn't you get it?"

Elias gave him a sideways grin. "I figured you deserved the honors."

"Whose side are you on?" Irritation mixed with hesitant curiosity hung in Ace's question.

"Ace, the sheer fact that you need to ask that says you don't know me at all. Miranda, please come downstairs with me," Elias said.

"This is like a nightmare I can't wake up from." If there were more criminals waiting, they'd never be able to fight them all. Randee retreated until her legs reached the end of the bed, and she dropped onto it.

The sound of men's voices carried from below.

"There's the rest of the party and the answers you want."

Elias walked over to where Malte was coming to. "I've waited a long time for this." He hoisted the man to his feet.

"The boy is dead! He's dead thanks to you, Steele!" Malte screeched.

"Diego is fine. Stop your bullying. Let's go." Elias dragged the shrieking man out the door.

"What's going on?" Ace walked to Randee. "Do we just let him take Malte out of here?"

"I don't know, and at this point, I'm afraid to ask." She pinched the bridge of her nose. "I guess there's nothing left to do but comply with Elias."

In a haze, she and Ace walked to the bathroom, where he retrieved Ghost from beneath the toilet lid. Then they trailed down the stairs.

As she stepped into the living room, she gaped at the front door standing wide open. Strobing blue and red lights approached, dancing in the darkness.

Yolanda stood, hands behind her back as an officer placed cuffs on her. The sight saddened Randee, and she longed to rush out of the house to defend the woman.

But she nearly came undone at the sight of the two men seated on the couch.

"Sergio? Wesley?" Randee gaped.

Ace gripped her arm. "Your team?"

She nodded, frozen in place.

"C'mon over here and have a seat," Sergio said, reaching out for her.

"She's gonna punch your lights out." Wesley chuckled.

Randee stiffened. "Someone better start explaining, and fast."

Several law enforcement personnel strode through the room.

"Miranda, please put down the pistol." Elias sighed, walking through the door.

She glanced down at the gun still in her grip and set it on the table. Ace helped her to the closest seat, a recliner facing Sergio, then sat on the adjacent chair, keeping close to her.

"I know you're angry, Jareau, but settle down," Sergio began.

Randee's emotions boiled, and her face grew hotter by the second. "I'm listening."

"Mr. Steele, my name is Sergio Vargas. I'm the special agent in charge, and this is Special Agent Wesley Zimmer." He addressed Randee. "Stop glaring at me like that."

She clenched her hands. "I'm so angry I can't think straight." Anger wasn't the word. Confusion? No. Fury. Pure fury. "You played me?" Her mind struggled to comprehend everything she was seeing. It wasn't possible. "I saw him dead." She pointed to Elias.

He tsked. "Actually, I was playin' possum."

She jumped to her feet. "How could you do that to me? I trusted you! I grieved your death!"

Sergio moved to her side and placed a hand on her shoulder. "Jareau, you need to hear us out."

"Hear you out? You tricked me. Was Yolanda in on all of this, too?"

"No, she wasn't. Ishi figured out Yolanda was the spy working for Malte. She also discovered he was using Diego as a way to control Yolanda. Her actions were understandable, but she will still be charged," Sergio said.

"I think we need to excuse Mr. Steele for the remainder of this discussion," Elias inserted.

Randee stood and moved beside Ace, placing her hands on the back of his chair. "No way. He's got every right to hear this, too. He's the only person in this room who hasn't betrayed me."

"Think before you speak, Miranda," Elias warned.

Randee crossed her arms over her chest and gritted her teeth. "Fine, I'm listening. What is going on?"

"The most dangerous thing an undercover agent can do is lose objectivity," Elias said.

Randee's ears warmed as she met Wesley's and Sergio's eyes. She wanted to dispute Elias's accusation but couldn't.

She had lost objectivity.

She had chosen Ace over justice, and she didn't regret it. But that wouldn't be what Elias or Sergio wanted to hear. Based on the humor in Wesley's eyes, he already knew.

Malte's belligerent voice emanated from outside where an officer was assisting the noncompliant man into the back seat of a police cruiser. Her gaze traveled, and she spotted Zeke sitting in a second car.

"Are all of Malte's cronies in custody?" she asked.

"There's more?" Wesley asked.

"Yeah, three others at PrimeRight," Ace offered.

"One's DOA," Randee said.

Wesley stood. "I'll notify the officers." He walked out the door.

"Why didn't you come and rescue us?" she demanded.

"You didn't need rescuing. We all know you're capable of handling yourself. And you did a great job, but your concentration was straying. We had to move fast. Ace was the only bargaining chip we had left," Sergio explained.

Randee couldn't believe her ears. "You used him as bait?"

Wesley returned and leaned against the wall, crossing his ankles. "We were running out of options, and we were too close to bringing down Malte. If we didn't flush him out of his hiding places, Ghost would've been transferred from his henchmen right to Malte."

"What about Fritz?" Ace asked.

"Nelson was always under protective care. He's been

in a medically induced coma to allow the swelling on his brain to reduce. Doctors say he's doing better, and they're optimistic he'll recover," Wesley replied.

Randee slumped into the chair again. "And Diego?"

"Diego is under 24-7 protection as well," Sergio said.

"That's a relief." Randee sighed. "So, when did I stop being apprised of the case?"

"When you left after the explosion with Ace, we knew you'd protect him, but we needed Malte. We had to draw him out. Ishi intercepted communication between Malte and his spy, Yolanda," Wesley said.

"Ishi dropped the clue about Elias's address to Yolanda. She delivered the information to Malte. We arranged for you to meet Ishi away from the property. Like a moth to a flame, Malte's henchmen showed up and ransacked the place looking for Ghost." Sergio placed his elbows on his knees and folded his hands.

"Thanks to Ace's quick thinking, he wasn't able to find it," Elias said. "Malte was searching for the briefcase, so removing everything was brilliant. He never considered anything other than a place big enough to conceal the case."

"But the medicine cabinet—" Ace interrupted.

"I did that for effect." Elias grinned.

"We knew Malte would stay underground and use his cronies to do the work. But he was getting antsy, too. After his men left, we added the photoshopped picture of Wesley and me, then we faked Elias's 'death' for you." Sergio used air quotes.

"That's why Malte was baffled when I questioned him about kidnapping you guys," Randee concluded.

"Yes. But he was running out of patience, and he was good at hiding. You did a great job of flushing him out."

Randee bolted to her feet, furious. "And why wasn't I apprised of this?"

"If you'd known, you could've blown our cover. You and Ace were getting too close. When I caught you kissing—" Elias started.

Heat rose up Randee's neck, and Wesley barely smothered his grin.

"—I knew you'd lost your impartiality. We were never certain of Ace's innocence or whether he was in cahoots with Yolanda," Elias concluded.

Sergio injected, "As bureau chief you must think globally. Not just about one person. Your concern for Ace is admirable but doesn't focus on the big picture."

Randee's shoulders slumped. They were right. She'd gotten too close. Blown it.

"You finally believe I'm innocent?" Ace asked.

"Yes, but Yolanda faces a slew of charges," Sergio confirmed.

"That's not fair. If she'd failed to do what Malte said, he would've killed Diego," Ace argued.

Wesley grunted. "No dispute there."

"If she'd contacted the ATF instead of taking matters into her own hands, we could've helped her," Sergio countered. "We understand the circumstances surrounding her decision, but she had other options. We could've protected Diego."

"A mother's love is fierce," Randee said defensively.

"But she broke the law. In a big way," Elias said.

"I'm sure you are anxious to be done with this. Steele, I'll take that from you." Sergio reached for the prototype.

Ace looked down. "This project has tested me at every level and been my worst nightmare and the best thing that ever happened to me." He passed Ghost to Sergio.

"Your only mistake was surrendering to your emotions.

Otherwise, you did a great job." Sergio gave her shoulder a squeeze, then he and Wesley exited the house.

The words were helpful but did little to defuse her anger still simmering at a low boil.

"Look, kid, I know you're mad. I get it. But you brought part of this on yourself. You have to know when your emotions are overriding your common sense. This case ended well, but had Ace Steele been working with Malte, you'd be in a deep pan of chili. Just like Yolanda will have to be held accountable for her choices, you would've faced the same predicament." Elias frowned at her. "However, Ursula and I shared many wonderful years together. I remember what it's like being in love. Clouds your judgment."

Randee gulped. In love? She jerked to look at Ace, then quickly averted her gaze. Elias was right. She was in love in Ace.

"Get out of here and get some rest."

"So, I'm clear? No longer enemy number one?" Ace asked.

Elias moved closer and seemed to study him. "You passed with flying colors, Steele. But take care of her. She's one in a million. Remember, I have a long memory and a lot of contacts." He winked at Randee, then stepped outside.

The remaining law enforcement personnel drifted out of the room, leaving her and Ace alone.

Ace turned to her. "Are you okay?"

She sighed, exhaling some of the irritated energy. "Yeah, Elias is right. I messed up." She glanced over her shoulder. "But I don't regret what I did. I followed my instincts, and they were right. I'd never have gotten to know you. That was worth whatever reprimand I receive over my actions. Ace, I have a confession." Her heart pounded, and an uncomfortable wave of vulnerability washed over her. Before she could stop herself, she blurted, "I am in love with you."

He stepped closer. "You are?"

She swallowed. Not the response she'd hoped for.

Ace placed a finger under her chin, lifting her face. "I think I fell in love with you on day one after seeing your mad fighting skills on those guys in the garage."

She grinned.

"But I don't act on emotions. As Elias said, they're not trustworthy or reliable sources."

His words sent a ripple of concern through her. Had his own confession of feelings been a result of being caught up in the moment? "I see."

"Let me finish. Instincts aren't quantifiable. I am a scientist, and if I recall correctly, you wanted to try an experiment to measure our danger-free chemistry." He took her hand and gently tugged her toward him.

Her pulse quickened. "Wouldn't you say that's really the only way to determine the results?"

"Absolutely. I believe finishing the kiss we started would be a great litmus test."

Randee's heart did a triple jump, and she met Ace's blue eyes. He tugged off his glasses, dropped them onto the chair and drew her close. She wrapped her arms around his neck.

The softness of his lips covered hers, gentle at first, tender and apprehensive.

Randee returned the kiss, deepening it. And the anger that she'd held on to only minutes before transitioned into a warmth that radiated from her shoes to her eyebrows.

When at last they parted, Ace set her gently on her feet. "What do you think? Was there any chemistry?"

Randee laughed. "I'm no scientific expert, but I'd say that was definitely a ten on the Richter scale."

He pulled her closer. "Hmm. All good scientific experiments require multiple tests to ensure reliable outcomes."

"That sounds like a lengthy process."

Ace nodded. "Yes, it does. Could take a lifetime to know for sure."

"Well, I hate to interfere with the progression of science."

"You're in good hands." He leaned in. "I love you, Miranda Jareau."

Randee drank in the blue of his irises. "I love you, too."

Ace enveloped her in a second kiss, gentle at first, that deepened with emotion and swept the ground out from beneath her feet.

Even if she'd lost her chances at a promotion, Ace Steele was worth the consequences. Who needed the burden of bureau chief, anyway?

EPILOGUE

Four months later

Impatience had Ace's knee bouncing at the lengthy event. Like all government agencies, the ATF dragged out the promotional ceremony for two grueling hours.

Sandwiched between Randee's mother, Marilyn—who shot him an annoyed glance—and Elias, who chuckled, he forced himself to stop fidgeting.

"Relax," Elias said, slapping him on the back.

"Right." Ace nodded.

When the ceremony concluded, Ace nearly bolted out of his chair.

After what seemed like an eternity, Randee made her way off the stage and worked a path through the congratulatory crowd with the grace of a rock star. Her approach reactivated his sweat glands, and he had to wipe his hands twice on his pants by the time she reached him.

Eager to embrace her, he didn't see Marilyn shove ahead of him until it was too late. Tamping down his annoyance at having to wait longer, Ace reminded himself that the slowly healing relationship between mother and daughter required droplets of compromise on everyone's part. Which was more than Ace could say for his own estranged family.

"Congratulations," Marilyn cooed, embracing Randee in an awkward hug.

"Mother. What a wonderful surprise. Thank you for coming." Randee shot him an apologetic and confused what-is-she-doing-here? look over her mother's shoulder.

He shrugged.

Elias interceded. "Marilyn, you've got to share her."

Her mother stepped back, clearly displeased by the intrusion. A measure of relief poured over Randee's face.

"Come here, kid." Elias hugged her. "I am so proud of you. Commendations for bravery on Malte's takedown and a promotion to the Denver office bureau chief. You stole the show."

Randee beamed at her mentor's praise. "It's everything I ever hoped for."

In his peripheral vision, Ace caught Marilyn bristling. Thankfully, Randee didn't seem to notice.

"Get on up here, Ace," Elias chastised.

Randee smothered a grin. Ace drew her close, whispering against her ear, "That took forever."

"I'm worth the wait," she replied, and leaned back, piercing his heart with her bright blue eyes.

Had she always been this beautiful? *Thank You, Lord.* "No dispute there." He kissed her full on the lips, ignoring the crowd and thrilled to hold her.

Too soon, Elias cleared his throat.

Ace reluctantly stepped aside, keeping his arm around Randee's waist.

"There she is." Ishi approached with the rest of her team and their wives.

"Congratulations to you, too." Ace reached out to shake Wesley's and Sergio's hands. "Big changes are coming."

Sergio took his hand first. "Thanks. Change seems to be the word of the year for all of us. Where's Fritz?"

Ace grimaced. "He sends his congrats and apologies. He wasn't able to attend because he received a last-minute offer to pitch a proposal in San Francisco. He took Diego and Yolanda along with a promise to sightsee and catch a game." The DA had worked out a deal for Yolanda. She'd serve probation for her part in Malte's plot.

"How's the new job going? What is it you do again?" Wesley asked.

"Thanks to Elias, I'm working for TSA in Denver doing weapons detection systems. It's amazing."

"My pleasure, Ace. You're a perfect fit for the position," Elias said.

"We figured you were trying to get rid of Ace by shipping him out of state," Wesley joked.

The statement was accurate, but Elias's insider knowledge had worked perfectly. He and the older man shared a knowing look.

"It'll take more than a little commute to break these two lovebirds up," Elias teased.

Marilyn tensed. She hadn't accepted him as part of Randee's life, but she was coming around. She'd even given her reluctant, but approving, blessing to the relationship.

"Take me along," Ishi teased.

Randee squeezed her friend's shoulder. "Visit anytime."

"You won't have ti—" Wesley's words were cut off by Larissa's not-so-subtle elbow jab to the ribs.

Randee clung to Ace's waist and gazed up at him. "This day cannot get any better."

"I can name a few ways," Wesley said, earning him a glower from Larissa. "Folks, I've been a good sport, but I'm hungry." He ushered the group away.

"Marilyn, would you do me the honor of joining me for the celebratory meal?" Elias asked.

Randee's mother almost cracked a smile. If Ace read

the whole situation correctly, there seemed to be a mutual attraction happening between them. "Thank you, Elias."

Randee tugged on Ace's arm. "We better get moving or there won't be anything left."

"Wait. I want a couple of minutes alone with you."

"Okay."

"I'm proud of you."

"Thank you for being so supportive."

"You did the same for me when I was offered the TSA position." He led her to a chair on the last row, ensuring her back faced the banquet hall where her team not so surreptitiously hovered in a corner, watching. No pressure. "I know this is already a big day, and you have a lot of changes to deal with."

"I can't believe Sergio and Elias recommended me for the Denver ATF office. Especially after everything I messed up with Ghost."

"You worked hard and showed them you're more than competent."

"Yeah, the endless assignments, paperwork and meetings kept me in a tornado of busyness. At least Sergio permitted me to continue working the case to the end after Malte's arrest."

"He saw you were capable, but for the record, I always knew." Ace inhaled her perfume. *Lord, I love this woman.*

"Our chemistry definitely outlasted the drama."

He sat beside her. "However, the experiment should continue for the purposes of long-term research."

She smiled. "When you moved to Denver, I worried about us having a long-distance relationship, but it hasn't been an issue. I mean, it's not ideal, but we've made it work. And now you know the city, so you'll be able to show me around and help me find an apartment when I move there."

He shook his head and ignored Wesley motioning him

to hurry up. "Actually, that's part of what I wanted to talk to you about. I don't think a new apartment is a good idea."

She paused. "Why?"

"Purchasing property is the best investment."

"Like a house?"

He nodded.

"Since when are you in favor of committing to real estate and payments?"

Ace knelt on one knee and removed the small ring box from his suit pocket.

Randee gasped as he displayed the emerald-cut solitaire in his palm. "I don't want to steal your thunder, but the past two months of commuting back and forth and not having you near me every day has been excruciating. I feel like I'm missing a part of my heart. Randee, I love you and I cannot spend another minute without you. Please say you'll be my wife."

She blinked, her blue eyes wide, and nodded emphatically. "Yes!" she said, jumping up.

Ace lifted and kissed her while her team applauded in the background.

Randee whispered, "So does this mean the experiment is a success?"

"Definitely." Ace took her into his arms and covered her lips with his kiss, sealing their future together forever.

* * * * *

*If you enjoyed this book,
look for these other stories by Sharee Stover:*

Secret Past
Silent Night Suspect

Dear Reader,

I am so grateful for you, and I appreciate your taking the time to read *Untraceable Evidence*.

After I've spent months with these characters, Ace and Randee have become near and dear to my heart. I hope you enjoyed getting to know them, too.

The biggest message they taught me through this story is that we don't have to be perfect for our heavenly Father. He's given us the greatest gift: grace. Freely given, not earned and lavished on us because we are accepted in the beloved. You and I are safe with God, even in our imperfection.

I enjoy hearing from my readers, so please connect with me on my website, www.shareestover.com, or drop me a line at authorshareestover@gmail.com.

Blessings to you,
Sharee Stover

WE HOPE YOU ENJOYED
THIS BOOK FROM

LOVE INSPIRED SUSPENSE
INSPIRATIONAL ROMANCE

Courage. Danger. Faith.

Find strength and determination in stories
of faith and love in the face of danger.

6 NEW BOOKS AVAILABLE EVERY MONTH!

COMING NEXT MONTH FROM
Love Inspired Suspense

Available June 2, 2020

DEADLY CONNECTION
True Blue K-9 Unit: Brooklyn • by Lenora Worth
On her way to question US Marshal Emmett Gage about a DNA match that implicates someone in his family in a cold case tied to a recent murder, Brooklyn K-9 officer Belle Montera is attacked. Now she must team up with Emmett to find the killer...before she becomes the next victim.

PLAIN REFUGE
Amish Country Justice • by Dana R. Lynn
After overhearing an illegal gun deal, Sophie Larson's sure of two things: her uncle's a dangerous crime boss...and he wants her dead. With a mole in the police force and Sophie in danger, undercover cop Aiden Forster has no choice but to blow his cover and hide her deep in Amish country.

SECRETS RESURFACED
Roughwater Ranch Cowboys • by Dana Mentink
When new evidence surfaces that the man her ex-boyfriend's father was accused of drowning is still alive, private investigator Dory Winslow's determined to find him. But working with Chad Jaggert—the father of her secret daughter—wasn't part of her plan. Can they survive the treacherous truth about the past?

TEXAS TWIN ABDUCTION
Cowboy Lawmen • by Virginia Vaughan
Waking up in a bullet-ridden car with a bag of cash and a deputy insisting she's his ex, Ashlee Taylor has no memory of what happened—or of Lawson Avery. But he's the only one she trusts as they try to restore her memory...and find her missing twin.

STOLEN CHILD
by Jane M. Choate
On leave from his deployment, army ranger Grey Nighthorse must track down his kidnapped daughter. But when he's shot at as soon as his investigation begins, he needs backup. And hiring former FBI agent Rachel Martin is his best chance at staying alive long enough to recover his little girl.

JUSTICE UNDERCOVER
by Connie Queen
Presumed-dead ex-US Marshal Kylie Stone goes undercover as a nanny for Texas Ranger Luke Dryden to find out who killed his sister—and the witness who'd been under Kylie's protection. But when someone tries to kidnap the twins in her care, she has to tell Luke the truth...and convince him to help her.

———————

LOOK FOR THESE AND OTHER LOVE INSPIRED BOOKS WHEREVER BOOKS ARE SOLD, INCLUDING MOST BOOKSTORES, SUPERMARKETS, DISCOUNT STORES AND DRUGSTORES.

LISCNM0520

Brooklyn K-9 Unit officer Belle Montera glanced back on the shortcut through Cadman Plaza Park, her K-9 partner, Justice, a sleek German shepherd, moving ahead of her as she held tightly to his leash. She had a weird sense she was being followed, but it had to be nothing.

Justice lifted his black nose and sniffed the humid air, then gave a soft woof. He might have seen a squirrel frolicking in the tall oaks, or he could have sensed Belle's agitation. Still on duty, she kept a keen eye on her surroundings.

"No time to go after innocent squirrels," she told Justice. "We're working, remember?"

Her faithful companion gave her a dark-eyed stare, his black K-9 unit protective vest cinched around his firm belly.

They were both on high alert.

"It's okay, boy," she said, giving Justice's shiny black-and-tan coat a soft rub. "Just my overactive imagination getting the best of me."

She had a meeting with a man who could have information regarding the McGregor murders. The DNA match from that case had indicated that US marshal Emmett Gage could be related to the killer.

The team had done a thorough background check on the marshal to eliminate him as a suspect, then Belle had been assigned to meet with him.

Justice lifted his head and sniffed again, his nose in the air. The big dog glanced back. Belle checked over her shoulder.

No one there.

She slowed and listened to hear if any footsteps hit the strip of pavement curving through the path toward the federal courthouse near the park.

Belle heard through the trees what sounded like a motorcycle revving, then nothing but the birds chirping. Minutes passed and then she heard a noise on the path, the crackle of a twig breaking, the slight shift of shoes hitting asphalt, a whiff of stale body odor wafting through the air. The hair on the back of her neck stood up and Belle knew then.

Someone is following me.

Don't miss
Deadly Connection *by Lenora Worth,*
available June 2020 wherever
Love Inspired Suspense books and ebooks are sold.

LoveInspired.com